ALWAYS

JOY AVERY

ALWAYS

Copyright© 2017 by Joy Avery

ALL RIGHTS RESERVED

First Print Edition: January 2018

DEDICATION

Dedicated to the dream.

DEAR READER,

As always, THANK YOU for your support of **#joyaveryromance**. I truly have some AMAZING and dedicated readers. You guys really know how to make this writer feel appreciated.

While **ALWAYS** concludes the Lassiter Sisters novella series, don't be surprised to see more from Mount Pleasance, North Carolina in the future. I hope you enjoy Sadona and Keith's love story. It's a tale of letting go of fear, doubt, and especially the past. The past can either help or hinder you. The choice is yours.

Please help me spread the word about ALWAYS by recommending it to friends and family, book clubs, social media and online forums. I'd also like to ask that you please take a moment to leave a review on the site where you purchased this novel. Reviews help to keep our love stories alive!

I love hearing from readers. Feel free to email me at: authorjoyavery@gmail.com

Until next time, HAPPY READING!

ACKNOWLEDGMENTS

To everyone who has supported me on this
glorious journey, THANK YOU!

1

Vanilla bean ice cream was no substitution for sex, but the double-scooped waffle cone brought Sadona Lassiter a great deal of pleasure. The sweet treat had been her way of celebrating a good week. A fantastic week, she corrected.

Earlier that week, she'd received her official divorce decree. Two days later, she reverted back to her maiden name. And just a few hours ago, she launched Carolina Lavender, the online skin care company she'd longed to start for years.

A smile touched her lips at the accomplishment. *No fear. No negative thoughts. No doubt. You've got this. You're going to rock this.* But with all of that said, she'd be the first to admit she was scared as hell of failing. *But you won't fail.*

The sensation of the melting ice cream rolling over her fingers garnered her attention.

"Shoot."

Taking her eyes off the road for only a second, she snagged one of the teal Mount Pleasance's Creamery napkins on the passenger's seat, then brought her focus back to the road...just in time to see the clump of fur standing in the middle of the road.

Dropping the cone and gripping the wheel, Sadona slammed on the brakes. A thick curtain of ash gray smoke kicked up behind the vehicle, then poured inside through the open sunroof—along with the rancid smell of burnt rubber. She coughed several times, the odor clogging her lungs.

When the vehicle came to a complete stop, Sadona took several moments to gather her thoughts, then another minute or two to scoop the wasted dessert from her lap. Finally exiting the vehicle, she ambled toward the front of the idling car.

Not wanting to get too close, she craned her neck to see around the front end. Her eyes landed on the unscathed dog standing there, panting as if he knew how close he'd come to becoming road kill.

"Not today, buddy," she said, then breathed a sigh of relief. All she needed was a dead dog on her conscience. "You're okay." She motioned in an attempt to urge the homely-looking animal to the side of the road and out of harm's way. When it didn't budge, she said, "You're not a cat. You don't have nine lives. Go on. You may not be so lucky the next time."

As if the creature understood her warning, it made an attempt to move. But when it placed its right front paw down on the asphalt, it yelped—in what Sadona took to be pain—then lifted the paw off the ground, allowing it to dangle in the air.

"Oh, no. You're hurt."

When the animal looked at her with the saddest puppy eyes she'd ever seen, her heart pitter-patted in her chest. Had it injured itself attempting to flee from her vehicle's path?

What was she going to do? She couldn't just leave him there. The idea of putting the matted animal in her car wasn't all that appealing. But it clearly needed medical attention. Planting a hand on her hip, she gnawed at the corner of her lip.

Between her rattled nerves and the scornful May sun beating down on her like a vengeful enemy, a bead of sweat rolled down the nape of her neck. At ninety-one degrees, she couldn't stand there all afternoon. The heat radiating from the asphalt only added to her discomfort.

"Ah-ha! I'll call animal control."

The brilliant idea faded a short time later when she remembered she'd intentionally left her cell phone sitting on the kitchen counter. She'd picked a heck of a time to decide she wanted to unplug from the world for a few hours.

"Okay, buddy. This is what we're going to do. I'm going to help you into my car and take you to the vet so that you can get that paw looked at. But we need to establish some ground rules first. No biting. No peeing. No pooping. You got it?"

Sadona rolled her eyes heavenward and shook her head. Was she really standing in the middle of the road on the hottest day of the year, thus far, talking to a dog that didn't understand a single word she was saying? But when the dog gave a single barked, she stared at him wide-eyed in amazement and reconsidered her previous thought.

"Good. Well, now that we've settled that, how in the heck are we going to get you from here to there," she said, eyeing the inside of the vehicle. She rested her hands on her hips. "Guess I'm going to have to carry you. You do remember our agreement, right? Especially the no biting part?"

Before she got another bark in response, a white, beat-up pickup truck puttered up the road, coming to a stop adjacent from her vehicle. An older gentleman with sun-aged, leather brown skin sat behind the wheel. When he popped the gearshift into Park, it sounded as if the engine would fall from the bottom of the jalopy. He adjusted the sweat-stained straw hat he wore, and his pale gray eyes startled her.

"Everything okay, darling?" he asked.

For some reason, the man's thick southern drawl made her smile. "Everything's fine."

His gaze lowered to the dog, then settled back on her.

"Well, all right, then."

He tipped his hat like a true southern gentleman, put the truck in Drive and puttered off. White smoke puffed from the tailpipe, and she hoped he'd make it to where ever it was he headed.

Refocusing on...Buddy...she decided to call him...she sighed. She held steady reservations about touching him. He looked as if he hadn't been washed in months. His wiry brown-black coat was stringy in some areas and matted in others. No telling what was buried under the unkempt fur. But when his stable front leg shook—probably from overcompensating for the injured one—she ignored her concerns.

Sadona knelt, but when she reached for Buddy, he cowered away from her. Had he expected her to strike him? Her heart broke at the idea of Buddy's previous owner abusing him. Questions rolled through her head. Had Buddy run away? Had his owner discarded him like trash to fend for himself? Had he wandered away from a loving family and not been able to find his way back home? She couldn't recall any lost dog signs posted around town.

Refocusing on Buddy, she said, "It's okay, fella. I won't hurt you. I promise."

Gently reaching for him again, Buddy allowed her to lift him. Holding him at arm's length, she carried him to the car and placed him on the passenger's side floor mat.

"Sorry, boy. This will have to do."

Buddy collapsed as though he were exhausted, then curled up into a tight ball. Sadona rounded the vehicle and slid behind the wheel. When the stench of unwashed dog filled her nostrils, she lowered all four windows.

Ten minutes later, they arrived at Mount Pleasance Veterinarian Clinic.

"All right, Buddy, we're here."

Buddy's head rose and his matted ears perked. Tilting his head, he eyed her as if he were curious about where *here* was.

"You're just too dang adorable. Too bad I can't keep you."

Now cradling him, she carried Buddy into the building. The uninspiring waiting room sat empty, which gave Sadona hope that she would be in and out. Maybe she'd replace her waffle cone. Approaching the front, she explained to the older, heavy-set woman sitting at the reception desk what had happened to Buddy.

Adda, the name tag she wore read. Her pecan-colored skin was speckled with tiny moles, and her honey-blond hair was fashioned in a mass of tiny curls. Something about the woman—possibly her stone-faced expression—told Sadona she was someone you didn't want to cross.

Adda led them to a room and informed her Dr. Fremont would be in shortly. Lowering Buddy to the floor, she scrutinized the small examination room. Three walls were painted a light gray color while the forth donned a lavender hue.

Black paw prints climbed from one corner and beat a path to the center of the wall. Several posters hung around the room. One about K-9 dental care, one displaying proper weight ratio for dogs, and another highlighting the importance of vaccinations.

Taking a seat, she blew out a heavy breath. A simple trip to the ice cream shop had turned into a trip to the vet. This was not how she'd intended to spend her Friday afternoon. She eyed the wet spot at her crotch where the ice cream cone had landed. To top things off, it looked as though she'd peed on herself.

She eyed Buddy. "Quit giving me those innocent puppy dog eyes."

A second later, Buddy curled at her feet. She leaned forward and picked a stem from his coat. "When was the last time you've been washed?" Or fed at that matter. Had he been vaccinated? Neutered? "I bet with a good grooming, you'd be—"

"Sorry to keep you waiting, Mrs. Lassiter."

"—the most handsome creature ever."

Sadona gasped at the timing of her words. Dr. Fremont eyed her quizzically for a moment, then smiled, revealing perfectly aligned and gleaming white teeth that contrasted nicely with his smooth dark brown skin.

Where was her cell phone when she needed it? This was a sneak-a-picture-and-send-it-to-her-sisters moment. Did forty-two-year-old women do such elementary things? Today, the answer was a resounding yes, because Dr. Fremont was fine and warranted sharing.

Tall—well over six feet. Strong, square jaw dusted with a five o'clock shadow. Pronounced Adam's apple. Broad shoulders. Lean, but sturdy. His dark brown eyes sparkled under the fluorescent lighting. She was sure that under the white lab coat his body was just as impressive as the rest of him.

Sadona didn't allow her eyes to travel beyond the red button-down shirt he wore. Taking in too much of the man could cause an adverse reaction. One that involved her nipples budding. How embarrassing would that be?

"Thank you," Dr. Fremont said.

His deep timbre snapped her from the dumbfounded state. "I was talking to the dog."

"Uh-huh," he said, flashing another brilliant smile—that viewed at the right angle could be considered wicked.

Wicked sounded like just what she needed. Snapping from her fantasies, she chastised herself. *Stop it, Sadona.* "Ms.," she said. When Dr. Fremont's brow shot up, she continued, "When you entered—in the midst of me talking to the dog," she clarified, "you addressed me as *Mrs.* It's Ms."

Oh God. Why did it sound as if she was trying to make sure he knew she was single?

"Ah. Well, my sincerest apologies, *Ms.* Lassiter."

They eyed one another in a not-quite-awkward but not-quite-relaxing manner. After several soul-stirring moments, Dr. Fremont slid his gaze away from her and eyed Buddy. When he knelt, Buddy inched closer to her.

"Uh-oh. Somebody's shy," he said.

Dr. Fremont appeared to be unaffected by Buddy's disheveled condition. He'd probably encountered far worse. While he made doggie chatter with Buddy, her eyes raked over the sturdily-put-together man, noting distinct things about him.

Perfectly proportioned lips. Laugh lines that creased his otherwise unblemished skin. The way his Adam's apple bobbed up and down. Why in the hell was that so appealing? His unshaven face didn't distract from his good looks. Actually, the ruggedness added to them. Everything about this man screamed trouble. The kinda trouble a girl who'd been forced to rely on her vibrator for the past year wouldn't mind getting into.

Her attention fell to the large hand he used to rub Buddy. Not that it mattered, but there was no wedding band on his finger. She couldn't explain it, but something fluttered in her stomach from the revelation.

With unhurried appreciation, her eyes crawled up his frame. She jerked when she discovered he'd been watching her. Her hand flew to the sterling silver heart pendant dangling from the chain around her neck. Fingering it, she said, "I'm sorry, did you say something?"

"I asked his name."

"Oh. Um…I don't know."

Dr. Fremont pushed his brows together. "You don't know your dog's name?"

Obviously, Adda hadn't told him everything. "Oh no. He's not *my* dog. I found him. Well, nearly hit him, actually. But I didn't," she made clear. "I noticed he was limping, so I brought him here. I've been calling him Buddy. He seems okay with it."

"Huh." Lifting Buddy, he pushed to his full height and carried him to the examining table.

Huh? What had that meant? When Buddy eyed her with those sad eyes and trembled, she joined them at the table. "Don't worry. I fully intend to cover the bill."

Dr. Fremont flashed another one of his confused looks.

"You said, 'huh.' I assumed you thought I planned to stiff you on the bill. I intend to pay."

"Do you do that a lot?" he asked, not looking up from his inspection of Buddy.

"What? Pay for strays?"

"No. Assume."

When those dazzling eyes settled on her, the swirl of desire inside her almost forced her to ignore his blatant cynicism.

Almost.

2

If her hard stare had been a knife, Keith Fremont would have been minced and scattered on the industrial tile under his feet. Still, her unyielding expression didn't force his eyes away. Partly because it took a little more than a scowl to spook him. But mainly because Sadona Lassiter was just so damn beautiful.

It had been a long time since he'd held an attraction this firm to any woman, not one that burned all the way down to the bone. A fact he'd been all right with. In his opinion, at forty-five, if settling down was in the cards for him, it would have already happened by now.

Being man enough to admit he'd possibly overstepped some line, he said, "I apologize," in an attempt to smooth her ruffled feathers. "I shouldn't have said that. Sometimes this mouth…"

His words trailed when her soft brown eyes lowered to his lips. It could have been his imagination, but he swore her breath had hitched. Her gaze lingered far too long to have been considered an innocent perusal. The way she ogled his mouth…there were thoughts.

Dirty thoughts.

Sinful thoughts.

Thoughts that probably mimicked his own—all the delicious ways he could use his tongue to please her.

In a flash, Sadona's eyes shot upward, pinning to his. Inwardly, he laughed at the mix of embarrassment and prideful indignation on her flawless brown face. This woman had a lot of fight in her, which drew him into her alluring pull even more.

Buddy whimpered and Sadona's features instantly softened. He might not have been her dog, but she'd clearly grown attached to him in the short time they'd been together. It was strange how dogs did that, made you fall in love with them with just one innocent look. Dogs never squandered and betrayed that love.

He tamped down the memory of his ex's betrayal when it worked its way into his thoughts. Three years should have been enough to purge all traces of her deception from his system, but it hadn't been. He wasn't sure a wound that deep would ever heal. But he prayed it would. He prayed one day he'd be able to forgive her.

To his dismay, Sadona broke their connection and slid her attention to Buddy.

"What's wrong, boy?" she said, rubbing his debris-strewn coat.

Keith liked the fact that Buddy's disheveled appearance hadn't detoured her from helping him. A big heart, and she liked dogs. Most women would have taken one look at him, turned up their nose and left him to suffer.

Compassionate. A quality he would want in a

woman—if he were in the market for love.

He scrambled the notion of possibly getting to know her. Besides, a woman as gorgeous as this one was probably happily married, or at least had a man or two waiting in the wings. Out of instinct, his eyes lowered to her left hand. No ring. 'Course, that didn't mean anything nowadays. Women were good at deceit.

Needing to put distance between himself and the cause of his rising temptation, he said, "I need to take Buddy to the back to run a few tests, if that's all right."

She nodded. "Sure. Whatever he needs."

For a brief moment, Keith toyed with the idea that Sadona had lied and had actually hit Buddy and was using generosity as some form of penance. *Nah*. If nothing else, she struck him as sincere.

"He'll be right back," Keith said, when it looked as if Sadona was suffering from separation anxiety.

The first person he ran into was Adda, which made sense, given the fact she was his only employee. That look on her face told him he was about to regret the next several minutes. Besides his assistant slash receptionist slash office manager, the woman was a notorious matchmaker, and like a surrogate mother to him.

"Shouldn't you be manning the front?" he asked.

Ignoring him, as she usually did, Adda trailed him to the back of the building. "She's gorgeous, right?"

"Hadn't really noticed."

Lies. All lies. Damn lies to be overly dramatic about it. Sadona Lassiter was exquisite. Did men even use that term? Didn't matter, because that's exactly what she was...exquisite. Something told him he wouldn't be able to forget the moment their eyes locked for the first time.

Free of makeup, her brown hair pulled back in a ponytail, a generic T-shirt, jeans—a wet spot at the crotch that suggested she'd been several seconds shy of reaching the bathroom—and flip-flops. Still, she dripped with beauty. How was that even possible?

Then it struck him. Maybe it wasn't her outer beauty he'd been attracted to. Maybe it had been her inner radiance that had garnered his attention. It took an individual with a good heart to want to help an injured animal. Especially one as battered by the elements as Buddy.

Adda planted her hands on her ample hips. "Hadn't noticed? Are you shitting me?"

Placing Buddy on the metal exam table, Keith tossed his head back in laughter. Adda never failed to call him out. The usually unfiltered and oftentimes brusque woman rarely held back her thoughts. And at sixty-something, hadn't she earned the right to speak her mind? "She's the gift that keeps on giving, son," his uncle had stated when Keith had taken over the practice a couple years ago.

"All right. Maybe I noticed a little bit." Who wouldn't have? Sadona displayed effortless beauty. That kind of natural radiance drew attention.

"You should ask her out."

How did he know that was coming next. "And why should I do that?" he asked, examining the laceration on Buddy's paw.

"Because you haven't stopped smiling since you walked out of the exam room."

"Couldn't my jovial display represent the love I have for my job?"

"It could. But unless you started just loving your job twenty minutes ago, I don't think so."

Never glancing up at the meddlesome woman, he said, "Adda Belle, why are you always trying to couple me up?"

"Because I love you like my own son and want to see you happy. *Truly* happy. Not that fake mess you force most days."

Her words melted the smile on Keith's face. He refused to make eye contact in fear of her seeing how close to home she'd hit. Adda wasn't the only one who wanted to see him happy again. He'd wished it for himself countless times. *Happy*. The concept seemed foreign to him at this point.

When Adda's warm hand rested on his forearm, Keith finally glanced up.

"You were dealt a shitty hand by a trifling woman. But all women aren't the same. The right one can change your life, change your heart. *Always* believe that."

17

Keith truly wanted to believe Adda, but what his ex had put him through with her lies— devastating lies—made him skeptical. An image of his ex chasing after him as he stormed down the hospital corridor burnt into his head. Swallowing hard, he forced the paralyzing moment away. That "right one" would have to have the thawing powers of the sun to reach that frozen muscular organ in his chest.

"Just think about it," Adda said.

To appease her, he gave a single nod.

Adda headed for the exit.

"Hey," Keith called out. When she turned, he said, "I love you, too."

She flashed one of her rare full-bodied smiles and continued out of the room.

Keith set his sights back on Buddy. "Hey, man, you're not going to tell your new mommy we were talking about her, are you? Bro code." Buddy barked and Keith laughed. "Good. Okay, let's see what we have here.

For the next half hour or so, Keith performed X-rays, drew blood, took a fecal sample and even gave Buddy a dime-store groom. Once he'd clipped away some of his rough coat, Buddy resembled an actual Border Terrier.

"Aren't you handsome. Your mommy's going to be thrilled by your new look. You ready to go see her?"

The second they reentered the room where they'd left Sadona waiting, her eyes bugged, and a

18

huge smile lit her beautiful face.

"Oh my God. Look at you," she said, bending to rub Buddy's tamed coat. "You look amazing. And much smaller."

At only ten pounds, Buddy was about six pounds underweight. But with proper diet, he'd be at a healthy weight in no time.

"Sorry it took so long," Keith said.

Returning to a full-stand, she said, "No problem."

Forcing his eyes away from her, he walked over to the table and placed Buddy atop it. "He has a laceration on the bottom of his paw, which had some infection. I gave him an antibiotic shot and a mild pain reliever."

"Laceration? How did that happen?"

"It could have been from digging, which Border Terriers are notorious for, or it could have happened when he was chasing something through the woods. Likely a squirrel. They're notorious for that, too."

"Oh," was all she said.

"I gave him several vaccinations. Surprisingly, he's in pretty good shape. A bit underweight, but nothing severe. There were no coat issues. I would recommend starting him on a monthly topical flea and tick preventative. We won't have the results from the fecal exam until later today, and the lab work until next week. I would like to start him on a de-wormer as a precaution. I'll give you a prescription…"

When Sadona's brows bunched, he allowed his words to trail. Apparently, so much information at once was overwhelming. He'd have Adda write everything down for her before she and Buddy left.

"You okay?" he asked.

"I can't keep him."

"Oh. I...just assumed—"

"Do you do that often? Assume?"

Sadona's sexy lips curled into a smile. His fingers tingled to touch hers. Refocusing, he chuckled. "I deserved that."

"I'm sorry. I couldn't resist."

A sense of humor. A quality he would want in a woman—if he were in the market for love.

Her gaze slid to Buddy. "Couldn't he belong to someone who's possibly looking for him?"

Keith shrugged. "More than likely he was abandoned when his owner could no longer care for him. If he were lost, most folk's first stop would be here to post signs. Unfortunately, he's not microchipped."

"People do that? Just toss their dogs out on the street?"

"You'd be surprised what people will do to animals." He'd seen some heinous shit. And since she appeared troubled enough, he didn't share any of them with her.

"What'll happen to him?"

"He'll go to a shelter and hopefully be placed for adoption."

"And if no one adopts him?"

"Unfortunately, he'll probably be euthanized." Which wasn't going to be Buddy's fate. Plus, he would never contact a kill-shelter. If he couldn't convince Sadona to take Buddy, he would. Baxter—his seventy-five-pound chocolate Labrador Retriever could use a playmate. However, he got the feeling Sadona really wanted Buddy. She just needed a little persuading.

Sadona's eyes rose urgently. "Couldn't you take him?"

"I would, but the only problem…" He massaged his stubble for effect.

"What?"

"My boy—my dog," he clarified, "has a nasty stomach bug. I wouldn't want Buddy exposed to it while he's recovering. His immune system is already compromised." He hated to speak illness onto Baxter, but it was for a good cause.

Rubbing Buddy's head, she said, "No, wouldn't want him getting sick," more to herself than Keith.

"I have an idea. If you can watch Buddy for the next two weeks, while Baxter recuperates, I'll give Buddy a permanent home."

An excited expression spread across her face, but faded a second later, replaced with one of worry. "I don't know. I mean, I want to, but I don't know anything about caring for a dog."

"You'll do fine. There's nothing to it." Making the offer even sweeter, he said, "And I won't charge you for today's visit."

She bit at the corner of her lip. "No, I better

not."

"Today's visit is $1500."

"But two weeks isn't really all that long. And he does seem to be well-behaved."

They both burst into laughter over her swift change of heart. Buddy's floppy ears perked, and he tossed a look between the two of them. Probably trying to figure out what the heck was wrong with the humans.

When things settled, Sadona said, "Is it really $1500?"

"No. I'm just messing with you."

"Whew. That's a relief. I literarily just started my own business and that would have been an expense I did not need."

"What kind?"

"What?"

"What kind of business did you start?"

"Oh. Skin care products. Carolinalavender.com." She shrugged. "If you want to check it out."

"I will."

"Great. I'm confident you'll find something your significant other will really like."

Was she fishing? Keith laughed to himself. Yes, she was. "Sounds good," he said, not revealing there was no significant other.

They eyed each other for a long time, which didn't bother him because he enjoyed looking at her. However, by the way she fingered the pendant on her necklace suggested their connection made her nervous. Why? Was the draw for her as strong as it was for him?

"Just two weeks?" she said, breaking the silence.

"That's it."

She contemplated another second or two before saying, "Okay."

"Excellent." He reached into his coat pocket and retrieved a business card. Writing his cell and home phone numbers on the back, he passed it to her. "Call me anytime." When Sadona flashed him an uncertain look, he added, "If you have any problems with Buddy."

Understanding unknotted her expression, and she accepted the card, sliding it into her pocket. "Well, I guess we should get going."

Why did he hate the idea of her leaving so much? "I'll walk you out." He lifted Buddy from the table.

"Thank you, Dr. Fremont."

"Keith, please."

She smiled and nodded. "Keith."

The sound of his name rolling off her lips was like a beautiful melody. He imagined her reciting his name over and over again as he made love to her. Something tightened in his stomach at the fantasy.

Trailing her from the room, his eyes roamed her body. Her ridiculous curves could cause the most skilled driver to lose control. And that ass. One of his hands subconsciously flexed as if tightening his fingers around her soft flesh. Why in the hell was he torturing himself like this?

Out front, Keith passed Buddy to Sadona, then grabbed a large bag of dog food. Following her to the vehicle, he loaded the food in the back seat, helped to get Buddy settled and held Sadona's car door for her.

"Enjoy the rest of your afternoon, *Ms*. Lassiter."

"Sadona, please." She flashed a lazy smile. "You, too, Keith. I'll see you in two weeks."

The question was, could he actually wait that long?

3

Keith bolted forward in his bed from the sound of the ringing house phone. His first instinct was to eye the clock. 1:21 a.m. The second was to slide a glance to the empty space beside him, as if Sadona would have been there. "You're insane, man."

He'd been having the best damn dream of his life. In the dream, Sadona's tempting body was stretched out across the king-size mattress, and he was kissing her from head to toe. Her soft moans of delight had floated through the air, swelling his ego.

The dream had been so real he swore he could taste her essence, smell it on his lips. A hunger rumbled in his stomach, and he adjusted his erection through his boxers.

Calls at this hour always bothered him, because they usually were preambles to bad news. Reaching for the cordless phone, he answered despite the words *private caller* flashing across the screen. "Hello?"

"Keith?"

He went still at the sound of the shaky voice on the opposite end of the line. *Sadona*. He sat up. "Hey. Everything okay?"

"No. I apologize for calling so late, but I didn't know what else to do."

"What's wrong?"

"Something is wrong with Buddy."

Like humans, dogs were susceptible to adverse reactions to medication, too, so his first thought was that Buddy had gotten sick.

"He's been whining for the past two hours. I've taken him out to use the bathroom several times, given him water, offered him food, fluffed his bed...nothing is working. He just keeps whining."

Keith swung his legs over the edge of the bed and planted his feet on the floor.

Sadona continued, "I even employed the tactic my sister uses for her nine-month-old and allowed him to whine. My nephew always dozes off after about ten minutes or so. Buddy has been at it for the past two hours. To the point he's losing his voice. Please help."

The exhaustion present in Sadona's tone made his next move a no-brainer. "Give me your address." Grabbing his cell phone from the nightstand, he keyed the address in. "I'll be right over."

"Oh God, thank you so much."

Without seeing her face, Keith could hear the smile in her voice. But she wasn't the only thrilled one. He'd thought about this woman since she'd pulled away from the clinic earlier. Seeing her was just what he needed. Though, he hated it was under these circumstances.

Standing, he reached heavenward to loosen his tight muscles, then headed into the bathroom.

After a quickie shower to wake himself up, he slid into a pair of dark denim jeans and a gray T-shirt, grabbed a few items he might need, then headed out the door.

After a quick stop by the clinic, Keith arrived at Sadona's place—a sage-colored, ranch-style house with a stone porch and stone and wood columns. A wicker rocking chair and sofa set occupied one side of the wide porch, while a potted tree claimed space on the opposite.

Moving to the front door, he rang the bell. Buddy's hoarse barks sounded. A second later, the cream-colored door inched open and a weary-looking Sadona peeped out, a cone-collared Buddy at her feet.

"Come in," she said, stepping aside. "Thank you so much for coming. Especially at this ridiculous hour. But I'm sure you're used to getting these types of emergency calls, right? If not, please say yes so I won't feel even more horrible about getting you out of your warm bed."

"Yes," Keith said. Which hadn't been a lie. However, he'd never made a house-call until now.

Sadona flashed a look of appreciation. Her tired eyes hinted at her need for sleep.

"I took his collar off thinking that could be the problem. But he started chewing on his bandages, so I had to replace it."

Keith had his suspicions about what ailed Buddy, but he did a quick check anyway to make sure there was nothing physically wrong with him.

Nothing. As suspected, the dog had suffered a bout of separation anxiety. Poor thing. He'd probably gone without direct human contact for so long that when he'd finally gotten it, he couldn't get enough. Just as they could with fear, dogs could also sense compassion. Sadona dripped with it. It had to be soothing to Buddy.

"Is he okay?" she asked, kneeling to rub Buddy.

"Yes. He just doesn't like you to be too far away from him."

Keith could totally relate. The woman's presence was like a warm fleece blanket on a nippy winter's night. Unable to stop them, his eyes roamed along her jawline, down her neck, over her shoulders, along her arms.

Refocusing, he pushed to a full stand before he lost control and pulled her into his arms and kissed her breathless. He would have enjoyed it immensely. He just wasn't sure if she would have approved.

"I swung by the clinic and grabbed acepromazine. A tranquilizer," he said when Sadona glanced up at him with a confused expression on her face.

"A tranquilizer." She stood. "They won't harm him, right?" She waved the words off. "Forget I asked that. Of course you wouldn't give him anything that would harm him."

"You're right. I wouldn't. It's mild. It'll just relax him. He needs some time to get used to his new surroundings. Temporary surroundings," he added. Though he had a feeling Buddy had indeed found his new permanent home.

Keith placed the pill into one of the pocket treats he'd also grabbed and offered it to an unsuspecting Buddy. The eager dog gobbled it right up, then ambled over to his makeshift bed— several folded blankets—and plopped down.

"If you don't mind, I'd like to hang around a few minutes to make sure he tolerates the medication okay."

"That would be great. Um...I mean, it would alleviate me having to phone you in another panic. Sorry about that, again."

If he hadn't known better, he would have thought Sadona relished the idea of him hanging around. "Quit apologizing. It's fine. Really."

Sadona led him to the couch and motion for him to take a seat. The ample space was boldly decorated in black, gray, and a yellow color scheme. It suited her. Strong, yet gentle around the edges.

"Would you care for something to drink? Wine, water, tea."

"Tea would be good."

"I'll be right back."

Several minutes later, she returned and passed him one of the two glasses she held.

"Are you not a drinker?" she asked, easing down onto the couch.

Keith hated the small strip of space between

them. He'd much rather they'd been sitting thigh-to-thigh. Better yet, her in his lap. He tingled below the waist at the thought. "Um…a social drinker. But I have to be at the clinic in a few hours."

Sadona rested her palm against her forehead. "Oh, no. I didn't even consider the fact you had to work tomorrow. Today," she corrected. Her hand fell. "Now, I really, really feel awful."

"We're only open until noon on Saturdays. I can get plenty of rest afterward."

"Good."

They eyed each other in cozy silence for a moment. Sadona tilted her head and narrowed her eyes.

"What?" he said.

"If I passed you on the street, I don't think I would have ever guessed you to be a veterinarian."

"Oh, yeah?"

She nodded.

"What would you have guessed?"

She shrugged. "Maybe CEO of a Fortune 500 company or a designer clothing model. You have a command-the-room type of look."

Her assessment completely surprised him. Sadona didn't strike him as the flirting type but it kind of felt as though that was precisely what she was doing. "Hmm. Thank you for the compliment."

There was a stark contrast between the woman who sat with her leg tucked under her ass now, and the frazzled beauty he'd encountered in his clinic the day before. This Sadona seemed relaxed, fun even.

Sadona took a sip from her glass. "So, how did you decide to become a vet?"

"My uncle. My father's brother. He raised me after my parents died in a boating accident when I was thirteen." He drank from his glass, unsure why he'd shared any of that with her. Even now, the memory of his parents' death affected him.

Sadona's voice was tender when she said, "I'm sorry. My parents are deceased, as well. I get it. The pain that creeps in when you talk about them. No matter how much time passes, it still hurts."

He nodded his understanding. "So, what did Sadona Lassiter do before Carolinalavender.com? Great site by the way. Very user-friendly."

"You checked me out?"

Keith bit back a roguish grin threatening to curl his lips. Oh, he'd checked her out plenty. Had damn near broken his eyes watching her escape to the kitchen. The way her ass had jiggled in those thin, pink cotton capris had convinced him she wasn't wearing panties. "Yes. Thoroughly."

"What do you think?"

"I can't wait to get my hands on you." He chuckled to downplay his intentional blunder. "On the items I purchased, I meant to say." Bringing his glass back to his lips, he said, "This is really great tea."

Sadona lowered her head, but not before he saw the lazy smile on her face. When it rose, her expression was back to neutral.

"Thank you. For the tea compliment and the purchase. I'm sure your girlfriend will love it. Full money-back guarantee if she doesn't."

It was the second time she'd gone fishing into his personal life. Again, he didn't correct her about the girlfriend statement. Was she interested in him? He leveled an assessing gaze on her. Apparently, she decided she didn't want him to burrow too deep into her telling eyes, because she turned away.

"Before I started Carolina Lavender, I did nothing." She studied the contents of her glass. Running her index finger around the rim, she continued, "My ex-husband liked the idea of me being a housewife."

"And you?"

She brought her gaze up. "I liked the idea of making him happy. Unfortunately, it was one-sided. He had an affair with a colleague. I left. And I'm not sure why I just told you any of that. You must think I'm insane."

"Resilient, actually. I can't imagine the strength it must have taken to walk away from the man you love."

"Used to love," she said. "And yes, it was hard, but necessary."

For the next half hour, they laughed, they talked—about everything under the sun. Their childhoods, their families, their life's bloopers. Keith couldn't believe how easy it was to talk to Sadona. They were like old friends who'd reconnected after years of being apart, without a single minute's lapse in familiarity.

They had a lot in common. A quality he would want in a woman—if he were… For some reason, he couldn't finish the sentence.

When they approached the subject of their exes, the mood shifted. He didn't offer much, but Sadona spoke freely. She grew sad talking about her past life with her ex. Alec was his name. She shared that the more power and prestige he'd garnered as a Fulton County Deputy District Attorney, the farther apart they grew. And how, even after the affair, she'd tried to make their marriage work. Until one day she'd stared into the mirror and told herself she deserved better.

Sadona placed her glass on the table in front of them and he followed suit. Silence descended on them. They carefully watched one another, studied one another, evaluated one another. He'd have paid handsomely to know what was flowing through her mind. And when the delicate expression on her face shifted to one of discernment, he had a feeling he was about to find out. But at what cost?

"Where are you?" she asked.

Confused by the question, he said, "Excuse me?"

"Black men. Where are you when we need you?"

Where had that come from? Instead of asking, he waited.

"Why aren't we ever enough? We live for you. Have died for you. Have postponed and abandoned our dreams to help you fulfill yours, because in our heads, your success will be our success."

Sadona went quiet for a moment, but watched him carefully. Had she been waiting for a response from him? Still, he remained silent. Not because he didn't have anything to say—quite the opposite—but because she needed to get this off her chest. All of it.

"It rarely works out that way," she continued. "When you make it, you forget about us and the sacrifices we've made to catapult you toward achievement. You walk into your new exclusive life as though we didn't help you get there. As if we never existed in your world."

Her words weren't scornful but were fully loaded. Despite her claim to no longer love her ex-husband, it was clear the pain of his betrayal still lingered. He had a suspicion this speech was directed more toward her ex, than black men in general, but he felt obligated to give a response.

"We're here. Society may have camouflaged some of us, but we're here. We've always been here. Eager to find you—our queens. Eager to cherish you—our backbones. Eager to be the kings you need us to be."

Sadona's eyes lowered briefly. When they settled on him again, they shined a little brighter. He wanted to believe he'd had something to do with that.

Continuing, he said, "We're here, Sadona. Waiting for our hearts to align with that one special woman who will make us *feel* like kings again. Some of us have been beaten down, too."

Sadona's brow crinkled slightly and a quizzical expression played on her face. She'd undoubtedly wanted to ask how he'd been beaten down, but the question never came—which had been a relief.

"You wonder where black men are; we sometimes wonder the same about black women."

"We're not hiding, Keith. We're somewhere picking up the pieces of our shattered dreams, hearts, in a society that often tells us we're less than, and a world where our men are constantly showing us."

Keith reclaimed his glass from the table and took a swig. He needed to fill his mouth before he let slip how he'd been left picking up pieces, too. Yes, she'd shared something intimate with him, but he couldn't talk about his past. Despite how comfortable he felt with her, he wasn't willing to give her that much of himself. Not yet. Maybe never.

"I'll get you a refill," Sadona said, reaching for the glass.

It happened so fast, it took Keith a second to realize he'd taken her hand into his. She flinched, and her gaze lowered to their joined fingers. His inner voice urged him to let go, but his brain refused to process the command. Heat pooled in his palm and tiny zaps of energy traveled up his arm. If she held any opposition to his touch, it didn't register on her face when she brought her eyes up to meet his.

"I'd forgotten how good it feels to have my hand held."

What else had she needed reminding of? Instead of asking, he took a wild guess—and a bold chance. Leaning forward, he delivered a single peck to her lips, then reared back to read her expression. When he didn't witness any protest, he touched his mouth to hers again. This time he didn't pull away.

Placing his free hand behind her neck, he deepened the kiss. Sadona's lips parted and welcomed his eager tongue inside. His kiss was greedy, yet thorough. Anxious, but complete. He hungrily claimed every drop of sweetness that lingered from the tea she'd drank.

Keith wasn't sure how long it had been since Sadona had kissed a man, but if it had indeed been a while, she hadn't lost her touch. As he devoured her mouth, explored every succulent inch, he questioned how far to go. Did she want him as badly as he wanted her?

But before things could progress beyond the point of kissing, Sadona's delicate hand pushed into his chest. Without hesitation, he freed her. He wished his body could have responded as quickly. Namely his erection, which threatened to burst through his zipper.

"I'm still picking up the pieces of me, Keith.

This won't go anywhere, can't go anywhere. Not now. I'm sorry if I... It just felt so..." Her eyes lowered briefly. "I didn't mean to lead you on."

He brushed a finger across her cheek. "You didn't lead me on. I kissed you, remember? If anything, I should be the one apologizing. You *could* even say I took advantage of you." That was a huge stretch, but he wanted to rid her of the unnecessary guilt she clearly felt. It was the gentlemanly thing to do. Especially since he'd nearly consumed her whole just a few minutes ago.

"No, you didn't. You can't force something that's wanted."

So she had wanted him to kiss her. Inwardly, he grinned. Unable to stop them, his eyes dipped to her mouth. Damn, he missed her lips already. The twitch in his pants was his cue to leave. The temptation was too high.

"I should go," he said, despite very much wanting to stay.

A faint hint of something flashed on her face. Disappointment? Nah. That would suggest she wanted him to stay, which contradicted what she'd just said: *This won't, can't go anywhere.*

"Oh. Um...okay."

The bemused look on her face made him entertain the idea that she wanted him to stay. No, if that was the case, she would have said so, right? Giving her hand a squeeze, he reluctantly released it and stood.

Sadona followed suit, resting the hand he'd

held in a fist against her mid-section.

Sliding his gaze away from her—before he did something ridiculous, like kiss her again—he focused on Buddy. "Somebody is knocked out. Looks like you just might get some sleep, after all."

"I'm not so sure about that," Sadona said.

She appeared to regret the words a second after their escape. Would the memory of their kiss hinder her rest? He had a good idea it would hamper his.

"I guess I'll see you in two weeks. Pending no more emergencies," Sadona said.

"I'm only a phone call away."

And he didn't just mean for doggie emergencies. For Sadona emergencies, too. That was a call he longed to receive, but was reasonably confident it would never come.

4

Sadona filled Rana's and her mugs with coffee, then poured a very pregnant Gadiya a large glass of orange juice. She loved when she could get with her sister. Especially today when she had so much on her mind.

The kitchen nook table overflowed with delicacies. When she hadn't been able to close her eyes without Keith's image burning into her head, she'd popped up at four that morning and baked muffins, cinnamon rolls, scones. She'd made a sausage casserole, fried bacon, and fresh-squeezed orange juice.

When she'd phoned her sisters at eight that morning, they'd both been eager to come over and help her dispose of the bounty. Especially Gadiya—who, since becoming pregnant, ate like she was going into hibernation.

"Sa-Sa, not that I'm ungrateful, but you only cook like this when you're stressed. What's wrong? Is Alec still trying to weasel his way back in?" Gadiya asked, stuffing almost an entire cinnamon roll into her mouth.

If her sister's consumption played any role in her soon-to-be niece or nephew's size, the baby was going to come out weighing twenty pounds, because Gadiya ate everything in sight. Amazingly, she hadn't gained an excessive amount of weight.

Good genes, she reckoned.

"Yeah, what's up?" Rana said, feasting on a strip of crispy bacon.

Sadona loved how her sisters knew her so well, how they knew each other so well. It was great at times, not so great at others—like when one was trying to keep something from the others.

"Other than my not being able to stop thinking about the man who kissed me in a manner I've never been kissed...nothing. Everything's fine." She didn't even bother addressing the Alec comment. Them reuniting would never happen.

Gadiya and Rana both froze mid-chew.

"Uh, what did you just say?" Rana asked, placing her bacon down to give Sadona her full attention.

"Yeah, because it sounded like you just said you've been playing lip-lock with someone," Gadiya added. "Someone who we..." she moved her hand between herself and Rana, "know nothing about."

Sadona gnawed at the corner of her lip, attempting to foil the smile twitching at her mouth from the memory of kissing Keith. There'd been some severe lip-locking all right. Keith had claimed her mouth in a way Alec never had. And her body had responded in a way it had never to a kiss.

"It just happened," Sadona said. "One minute we're talking, the next...his mouth covered mine. God, the way he kissed me set my entire body on fire. It was...perfect." Perfect was a term she rarely used, but it was the one word that could adequately describe their kiss.

"Oh my God! You slept with him," Gadiya said, her eyes wide with excitement.

"No, I didn't," Sadona said, less enthusiastic than her sister. "But I wanted to. I really wanted to. I really, really wanted to. It's been sooo long." Well over a year. She'd wanted Keith—needed him—to quench the thirst inside her before she dehydrated. It hadn't happened.

"Why didn't you sleep with him?" Rana asked. "That one-night-stand stigma is so antiquated."

"Oh, trust me. I would not have had a problem with it."

Rana's brow quirked. "So what happened?"

"He left."

"Sadona Lassiter, what did you do?" Rana asked.

Before Sadona could respond, Gadiya waved a hand through the air.

"Okay, wait. Let's rewind. Who is *he* and why in the hell—" Gadiya stopped abruptly, rubbed her stomach, then continued, "Why in the *heck* did he leave?"

Obviously, Gadiya hadn't wanted the baby to hear any bad words in the womb.

"Keith Fremont." A tingle fluttered in her belly at the mention of his name. "Buddy's vet." And the man who'd taken the art of temptation to a whole 'nother level.

Hearing his name, Buddy's head rose from his position curled next to Gadiya's chair. He'd loitered around the table the second they'd all sat down, clearly with hopes of scoring some table scraps. Sadona had warned Gadiya against giving him any, but the second he'd flashed those innocent puppy eyes at her, Gadiya had slipped him a corner of a muffin and had instantly become his BFF.

"What did you do?" Gadiya and Rana asked in unison.

"Why do I have to have done something?" Sadona countered. When they gave her the we-know-you stare-down, Sadona chuckled. "Okay, I may have made it sound as if I wanted him to leave."

"What did you say?" Rana asked.

"Something along the lines of 'this won't and can't go anywhere'. Then I apologized for leading him on. But I hadn't been referring to what we had been doing. I'd meant us—a relationship." Saying it aloud, she understood why he'd left—probably confused as hell. She'd sounded like a crazy woman. "I should have been clearer." She sighed again, this time heavier. "But anyway... Missed opportunities," she said.

"I'm confused. We can contribute it to pregnancy brain. Why can't it go anywhere? You are free to entertain a new relationship. Your divorce is final. You can't hide behind that mask any longer, big sis."

Hide? She hadn't been hiding. She and Alec had been separated and going through a divorce. Which for her meant she'd still been a married woman. Yes, she'd turned down numerous invitations to coffee, dinner, movies. But despite Alec's infidelity, she'd chosen to continue to honor the vows she'd taken until their marriage had been officially dissolved. She didn't regret the decision she'd made.

She wasn't sure—scratch that—she *knew* she wasn't ready to risk her heart again. Not to mention the fact her trust meter needed some serious recharging. Plus, Keith was a good-looking doctor. That reeked of disaster. Women loved handsome medical professionals.

"Why does it even have to be about things going anywhere at all?" Rana said. "You can just focus on simply enjoying each other's company. No strings attached. And what happens, happens."

"By enjoying each other's company, she means you enjoying his dick and him enjoying your p—"

"Gadiya Lassiter Dupree!" Sadona warned.

Gadiya rested a hand on her chest. "What? I was going to say presence. Get your mind out of the gutter, Sa-Sa. On second thought, keep it there."

Rana laughed. "Whew. For a second there, I thought you were about to say pu—"

"Rana Lassiter Fontaine!" Sadona reached over and rubbed Gadiya's protruding belly. "Not in front of the unborn child. And always remember, you are ladies."

All three women burst into laughter at Sadona

reciting one of their mother's constant reminders.

"I miss mommy," Sadona said.

"I miss daddy," Rana said.

"I miss Phoenix," Gadiya said, her bottom lip trembling slightly. "I visited their graves yesterday to replace the flowers we placed last week."

It always gave Sadona pause when Gadiya visited their parents' and brother's graves. Up until a year or so ago, Gadiya bad been unable to even step foot near the cemetery. *Nico*, Sadona thought. The man had been so good for her sister.

Sadona moved passed the solemn moment, reached out and placed her hand on Gadiya's belly. "It's okay, niece or nephew. Auntie Sa-Sa is looking out for you in front of your wayward mother and auntie."

The room filled with laughter again.

"Okay, back to Dr. Fremont," Rana said. "If the way you lit up when you said his name is any indication, he's definitely a job you should apply for."

Sadona was sure Keith offered a few positions that would please her. And there was no doubt he came with an *excellent* benefits package. She'd peeped that last night on the couch when she'd caught sight of the impressive bulge in his pants after their kiss.

"Yep, she wants him," Gadiya said. "She's fantasizing about him right now."

"Am not," Sadona said, swatting at her sister.

For the next couple of hours, the three

women chatted about everything: life, liberty, happiness, men. Especially men. Sadona loved spending time with her besties. Without her sisters, she would have been lost during her divorce. Thank God for family.

Gadiya flashed a pained expression. "I have to go, sissies. I have Lamaze class in a couple of hours. But first, I need my husband to scratch this itch." She struggled to her feet. "Pregnancy has turned me into a nympho."

"TMI," Sadona said, standing and moving to the cabinet. "I'll pack you a to-go baggie."

"I have to go, too," Rana said. "I didn't pump before I left the house. My boobs are aching," she said, cupping her breasts.

"Umm, totally TMI," Sadona said.

More laughter spilled from them.

Sadona paused a moment and observed her chatting sisters. She couldn't help but smile when she saw how happy they both were. Especially Rana. She and her husband Dallas had gone through a lot, but they'd come out of it stronger than ever. Thankfully, Dallas had come out of the ordeal cancer-free.

Gadiya had gone through something horrible, too. She'd come close to losing her husband Nico in a building fire when he'd gone inside to rescue a colleague and had become trapped. *Thank God for Greenville*, she thought, referring to the man who'd led the two men to safety.

She was overjoyed for her sisters and the love

they'd both found. True love. Unconditional love. That's what she wanted one day—true and unconditional. A love that wasn't contingent on her being a certain size or her looking and dressing a certain way.

Every time she observed her sisters with their husbands—the warmth, the admiration that danced in the men's eyes when they looked at their wives—revealed to Sadona that something had been severely lacking in her marriage. Authenticity. Honestly, she and Alec should have ended things a while ago. But she'd held out hope that things would get better. They never had. Despite how lonely she was, Sadona never once regretted her decision to leave.

"Sa-Sa..." Gadiya started.

"You okay?" Rana completed.

Sadona forced a smile, because that was what she always did—displayed strength she didn't always feel. "Yes. I just love seeing the two of you so happy."

"And we want to see you happy, too," Rana said.

"Yeah, and not that pretend happy thing you do," Gadiya said, then hugged her as best she could with her protruding stomach in the way. "We know you're lonely."

Dang. Had it been that obvious? This was one of those times when her sisters knowing her so well was a nuisance.

Gadiya continued, "Maybe this Dr. Fremont

character is just the distraction you need."

Sadona didn't bother to argue. Maybe she did need an interruption in her monotonous life. Keith could be just the disturbance she needed.

***

"Love is a vicious beast, man. That's why I avoid it at all costs."

Keith laughed at his best friend Craven Monroe. Craven was one of the first people he'd met when he moved to Mount Pleasant from Virginia. The man entertained his fair share of women, but not one had been able to wrangle the self-proclaimed eternal bachelor's heart. Outside of his lethal ability to charm the bloomers off a nun, Craven was the best mechanic in a hundred mile radius.

"No one said anything about love. I just...can't stop thinking about her," Keith said. For the past week, Sadona had danced a two-step in his head.

Craven slid from under the Honda SUV he was working on. "Same thing." Sliding back under the vehicle, he said, "If you like this woman, and clearly you do, pursue it."

Keith chuckled. "Nah. She made it pretty clear she's not looking for anything serious."

"Are you?"

A week and a half ago the answer to the question would have been a resounding no. Hell no, actually. But now... To be honest, he didn't know what he was looking for. The fact that Sadona could so easily affect him gave him pause. He hadn't even experienced this level of desire and attraction to his ex—and she'd given him a son. *And taken him away*, he added.

Keith washed a hand over his head. "Man, I don't know. After what Elena did to me, I swore I'd never let another woman—" He stopped abruptly when suppressed anger bubbled up inside of him. Tamping it down, he continued, "But this woman… She's in my system, and I can't seem to get her out. And all we did was kiss." A kiss that had awakened something that had lain dormant inside of him for years. Need. "We just met, but I feel like I've known her all my life."

Keith didn't want to think about Sadona, but he didn't want to forget her either. Couldn't forget her. His body made sure of that every time he put anything sweet into his mouth. He released a tortured sound.

Craven slid from under the vehicle again, this time sitting up. He removed a grease and grime covered rag from his oil-stained dark gray mechanic's onesie and added more crud from his hands to it. A black smudge streaked across his right cheek. Dreads that usually hung midway down his back were now fashioned in one thick braid.

"Damn," Craven said. "This woman must be something special. I don't think I've ever seen you this frazzled.

"Yeah, well, it doesn't matter. She's unavailable. So…"

"Friends before lovers, dude."

Keith massaged his jaw. "What does that mean?" Actually, he knew what it meant but wanted to know how it pertained to his situation.

"She may not be ready for a relationship, but everyone needs a friend." He winked. "Let her get to know you. Once she does, she'll warm up to your knucklehead. You're a real likable dude. After that, you'll be in there. If that's what you really want."

Keith laughed at his friend when the man shivered as though the idea of being in a relationship was the worst atrocity known to man.

"Seriously, man. You're a good brother. And if this woman has this kind of hold on you…" Craven shrugged, "then maybe it's something you should explore."

Keith chuckled. "For someone who avoids relationships like the plague, you sound awfully knowledgeable."

"I avoid love, I didn't say I've never been in it."

A look of sadness flashed in Craven's eyes. A second later he turned away and absently stared off as though he remembered a sentimental time in his past. Snapping out of his trance, he stood and tossed the tattered rag atop a tool-strewn cart. "Trust me. Work the friend angle. And if it's meant to be, things will fall into place."

Work the friend angle. Why did the words

sound so deceptive? Keith checked his watch. "Shit. I have to go," he said, standing from the mechanic's creeper seat he'd been sitting on. "Duty calls."

"Dude, you really need to hire another vet."

"Working on it. I have an interview with a promising candidate next week."

The two men fist bumped, then made plans to hang out soon.

On the drive back to the clinic, Keith couldn't get Craven's words out of his head. *Work the friend angle*. Could he and Sadona even be considered friends? They barely knew each other. He barked a laugh. *I obviously knew her well enough to slide my tongue down her throat.*

That damn kiss.

Something blossomed in his chest at the thought of their soul-stirring connection. A kiss that still had his brain and body scrambled. A kiss that would haunt him until he was allowed to taste her mouth again. And if that were never, the kiss that would haunt him to death.

When Keith walked into the clinic, Adda cornered him. In a hushed voice, she said, "Lady Cray-Cray is in exam room one. Swore it was an emergency, as usual." Adda rolled her eyes heavenward. "Says one of the '*boys*,'" Adda made air-quotes, "is feeling irregular. She must have given him some of her nasty-ass banana pudding."

Only one person fit this bill. Mrs. Augustine. The woman had fifty cats she treated like children.

At least three times a week, she bought one of her *boys* in for some nonexistent ailment, but he entertained her. Plus, she referred all of her animal-loving friends to his practice.

The thought of anything from her kitchen made Keith shiver. The last time she'd been there, she'd brought him some of her *to-die-for banana pudding*. Accidentally dropping the container, it spilled all over the kitchen floor. Baxter had been on top of it, nearly defying speed to get to it. But when Baxter took a whiff, he growled, barked at it, then took off down the hall.

"Be nice, Adda Belle."

"Did you do what I told you to do?" she asked.

"What was it you told me to do again?" he asked, not as clueless as he pretended to be. Before leaving for lunch, Adda had all but ordered him to contact Sadona and ask her out.

Adda socked him in the arm. "Don't play dumb."

He rubbed his arm and pretended to be in pain. "Ow. Is violence necessary?"

Adda tried to bite back a laugh, but it broke through. "Get away from me, boy, and go check on the crazy cat lady."

Keith parted his lips to give another warning, but Adda spoke before he could.

"I know. Be nice. Yadda, yadda, yadda. Call Sadona."

"Maybe I will. Maybe I won't."

With a wave of the hand, Adda dismissed him.

Keith laughed and headed down the hall toward the exam room. Heck, he couldn't handle the one woman he had in his life. What would he do with two? Giving it further thought, he might not be able to handle Adda Belle Chisholm, but he sure as hell could handle Sadona Lassiter's sexy ass.

5

Sadona finished packing the several orders that had come in over the past week, including the one Keith had placed. Almost three hundred dollars in assorted items. Lavender bath bombs, coconut lime foot scrub, whipped coconut oil body butter, an exfoliating loofah, and several more items.

Yes, men could use her products, but something told her Keith wasn't the cucumber mint sugar scrub type. So who was he purchasing the items for? Considering the kiss they'd shared—she shivered at the thought—he didn't have a significant other. At least, she hoped he wasn't *that* kind of guy. There wasn't a ring, which suggested no wife. His mother was deceased. So, who—

She abruptly ended the thought. Didn't matter. All that mattered was his payment had cleared. Still, the lingering mystery nagged her. And so did the fact that she'd lifted her cell phone roughly seventeen times in the past hour to call him, but had chickened out every time.

What was the harm in inviting the man out for coffee? As friends, of course. Just friends. There would be no holding hands—despite how great it had felt previously. There would be no kissing—regardless of how much her lips tingled for his. There would be no sex. Definitely no sex—she didn't care how defiant her body became.

They would start there. As friends. And if by chance it led to more, then so be it. She wouldn't push, but she wouldn't pull either. She would just go with the flow.

As tempting as a friends with benefits arrangement sounded, she wasn't crafted for casual sex. She felt things too deeply. A curse and a blessing. Mainly a curse.

Buddy sauntered into the room and stared at her. "You ready for your walk, fella?"

His tail wagged.

"Can you give me five minutes?"

He barked once, then ambled from the room. Lord, she swore that dog could understand her.

Buddy was another reason why she needed to figure out whether or not she would ask Keith to coffee. Either way, she would have to call him soon to tell him she'd decided to keep Buddy. The dog had grown on her. Buddy had brought her a level of happiness she couldn't explain, just feel.

Sadona had a sneaky suspicion that this had been Keith's plan all along, to make her fall in love with Buddy. If so, it had worked. The dog was like the child Alec never had the time—or desire—to give her.

Her cell phone rang, and she blindly answered. "Hello?"

"Hey."

The smooth baritone voice on the opposite end stilled her. Speak of the devil. Why was Alec calling her? Though she harbored no ill-will toward her ex-husband, they couldn't exactly be considered friends.

"Sadona, are you there?"

Snapping back to the conversation, she said, "Yes."

"How are you?" he asked.

"Well. And yourself."

"Good. I'm good."

Silence fell between them. History suggested Alec was building to tell her something. No doubt something that—in the past—would have hurt her. Fortunately, she was fairly certain there was nothing he could say that would have any effect on her now.

"I'm getting married, Sadona. I wanted you to hear it from me instead of someone else."

No effect at all.

Whom would she have possibly heard this news from? All of her so-called friends had shunned her after the separation. Had he really contacted her out of goodwill, or had he wanted to rub his impending nuptials in her face. A way of getting back at her for leaving him. Though she was sure he'd told everyone it was the other way around. And they'd probably believed it.

Sadona would have been lying if she'd said the information hadn't jarred her slightly. They hadn't even been divorced a full month and this fool was remarrying. Clearly, he hadn't shown her the same respect she'd shown him. He'd carried on as a single man while she'd done the right thing and waited until there was a divorce decree in hand. But why should she have expected more from a man who cheated on his wife?

"Congratulations, Alec. I'm happy for you." And she'd genuinely meant it.

"Really? I mean, I know it's sudden, but with the baby coming, we—" Alec stopped abruptly, obviously realizing he'd said too much.

Whether she liked it or not, *this* had an effect. "Baby? She's...pregnant? With *your* child?"

Alec's tone was guarded when he spoke, "Sadona—"

"Don't, Alec." Unshed tears stung her eyes. "Don't you dare attempt to pacify me." Her voice cracked. "You bastard. You—"

He sighed heavily. "This is exactly why I didn't want to tell you. I knew—"

She slapped a single tear from her cheek. "You knew what? That I'd call you out on the fact that for years I begged you to have a child. *Begged* you, Alec. But it was never the right time. Excuse after fucking excuse. Now you call and *accidentally* tell me you got some...some," there were several harsh labels bouncing around in her head, but she took a higher road, "*woman* pregnant while we were still married."

If she were standing in front of him, Sadona was sure Alec's head would be hung low and his hand washing back and forth over his head.

God, what was she doing? There was no way she should be allowing him to have this much power over her still. Taking a deep, cleansing breath, she said. "I wish you well in your new life, Alec. There's no reason for you to ever contact me again. Goodbye."

Without waiting for his response, she disconnected the call. Closing her eyes, she calmed her mind. Nothing Alec did should surprise her— including getting someone pregnant. Admittedly, the news hurt more than it stunned, but there was no need to dwell on it any further. She'd had her moment. Now it was time to move beyond it.

"Despite everything, life goes on," she said, echoing one of her late mother's favorite sayings. "Yes, it does, Mommy."

As if sensing something was wrong, Buddy ambled into the room. Seeing him, her mood instantly improved. "No way am I getting rid of you," she said, bending to pick him up. "Are you ready for your walk?"

Buddy licked her cheek.

"Well, let's go."

The walk to the square gave Sadona plenty of time to think, and she'd come to a conclusion. "I'm going to do it," she said aloud. She was going to ask Keith to coffee. Strangely enough, Alec's news had given her courage. The worst he could say was no to her invite. It wouldn't be the end of the world.

Pulling her phone from her pocket, she pressed the speed dial number associated with his name, then placed the device to her ear. Unfortunately, the call went directly to voicemail.

"Um...hi, Keith. It's Sadona. Sadona Lassiter." She paused, second-guessing herself briefly. "I was wondering if—"

Sadona stopped when her gaze drifted through the large window of the Mount Pleasance Bakery across the square. Her eyes narrowed as recognition set in. *Keith.* Sitting at one of the inside sunlight tables—as Janice Randall, owner of the bakery, called it. And he wasn't alone.

Could she be who he'd placed the skincare order for? Probably. A ting of jealousy, then anger rippled through Sadona.

"Never mind," she said, ending the call.

Entranced, she observed the two together. When the brown-skinned brunette tossed her head back in laughter, she wondered what funny thing Keith had said to elicit such a reaction. Before she could invest too much energy in speculating, Buddy took off across the lawn, yanking the leash from her hand.

"Buddy, no! Stop. Come back."

She charged after him, but the dog was like a cheetah on acid. He darted to the left, to the right, then sprinted toward her and dashed right through her legs. She attempted to step on the leash but wasn't fast enough.

Rushing after him again, she said, "This is so not funny, Buddy. You come here right now."

Unfortunately, he was far more entertained by the countless squirrels racing around than by her need to corral him.

Ugh.
This was all Keith's fault.

***

So far, Keith was impressed with Presley Andersen and had a feeling she'd fit right in at the clinic. More importantly, he had a feeling she'd fit right in with Adda. Also, her resume was impressive. She'd attended the College of Veterinary Medicine at North Carolina State University, graduated top of her class, had experience in emergency and critical care.

"The position…" His words trailed when he realized Presley's attention was elsewhere.

"We should probably help her," Presley said, her gaze set out the large window.

He followed her stare across the square. A woman in a navy blue tee and khaki shorts sprinted across the grass. Wait. He eyeballed the frantic woman. *Couldn't be*. He spotted Buddy in a triathlon-worthy sprint. It was. Sadona.

"I got it," he said, lunging from his chair. Keith darted through the exit and across the street.

Sadona chasing a determined-to-catch-a-squirrel Buddy, yelling and flailing her arms, had to be the funniest thing he'd seen all year. However, he kept his amusement to himself. When Buddy turned on a dime and dashed past her, Sadona attempted to step on the leash. Unfortunately, she lost her footing and toppled ass-first onto the grass.

Instead of pursuing Buddy, he chose to check on her first. He knelt. "Are you okay?"

"This is all your fault," she spat, slapping nonexistence debris from her smooth brown thighs.

Keith's head jerked back. Arching a brow, he said, "My fault? How is this my fault?"

This should be good.

Sadona glanced toward the bakery. It was subtle, but her jaw clenched. *Interesting.*

A beat later, she returned her gaze to him. "Never mind." Her words came in a low, tight tone.

Oddly, she seemed upset with him. But what possible reason could she have to be? She shot another quick glance toward the bakery before pushing up from the ground.

"Let me help you," he said, cupping her elbow. Her skin was damp with perspiration and as soft as he remembered. His fingers yearned to blaze a path up her arm, over her shoulders, and behind her neck to pull her mouth to his. Too bad that wasn't an option.

Or was it?

Sadona inched her elbow away. "I've got it, but thank you."

On her feet, she dusted her backside off. He tried his best not to appreciate the way her butt cheeks jiggled a little each time she swatted them. A knot tightened low in his stomach just thinking about how perfectly they would fit in his hands. If he performed a search for sexual torture, he was sure an image of Sadona Lassiter would be there.

When she eyed him, her cheeks glowed with a faint red hue as if she were blushing. If he had to guess, she was more flustered than embarrassed.

"Can you please help me catch this dog?" she said, resting a hand against her forehead, her tone much softer.

"Of course. How'd he get away?"

"He yanked the leash from my hand. I was distracted."

She seemed to regret adding the latter the second the words passed over her glossy lips. Lips he desperately wanted to experience again and again and again.

Tempted to inquire about said distraction, he focused instead on wrangling a full-throttled Buddy. Finally getting hold of the energetic dog, he led him back to Sadona and handed over the brown leather leash.

"Thank you so much," she said. "I read you're not supposed to say..." her voice lowered, "'*bad dog*, but I'm certainly thinking about it."

Keith knelt and rubbed Buddy. "He's not bad. Just doing what's in his nature. With all the squirrels racing around, this is like a theme park for him. Isn't that right, boy?"

Buddy's tail wagged so vigorously, his entire backside shook.

"Thank you again for the help. Don't let me keep you from your lunch companion," Sadona said. "I think she's eager for your return."

Keith sent a glance in the direction of the bakery. Presley stood outside on the sidewalk, staring in their direction. He came to his full height, eyeing Sadona a second or two before speaking— captivated by her effortless beauty. "Yeah, I probably should get back. Wouldn't want to make a bad impression."

"First date?" Sadona asked.

Keith swore he'd heard Sadona's teeth grit. He'd definitely witnessed a hardening of her expression.

Interesting.

"An interview," he said.

Something innocent twinkled in Sadona's eyes and an unmistakable look of relief spread across her face.

Interesting.

Sadona's brows bunched. "Interview?"

"Yeah. I'm looking for another veterinarian to join the practice. Free up some of my time for...other things."

"Oh. I...mean, that's great. Wonderful. Right?"

"I'm not sure yet. I have no idea how to react to the idea of excess free time."

"Well, I could use an assistant if you *really* need something to do."

Sadona smiled and it lit his world. "Anytime," he said. "You have my number."

They stood in comfortable silence for a moment. Damn. This woman made his imagination run buck-wild. He already knew how it felt to kiss her, but he wanted—needed—to experience and explore more of her. Much more.

When he stirred below the waist, he snapped out of his trance. He pointed over his shoulder. "I should go." Because she was becoming a serious distraction.

"Okay. Thank you, again, Keith. I really appreciate it."

"Glad I could help. Enjoy the rest of your day." His eyes lowered to Buddy. "And you behave."

Buddy gave a single bark, and they both laughed.

Keith started away, but stopped and faced Sadona again. "I'm curious. What had you so distracted?"

He was a hundred and ten percent sure she hadn't meant for her eyes to slide toward the bakery, but they did. Strange how your body performed involuntary actions against your will. And usually when you least expected and certainly didn't want it.

Refocusing on him, she said, "I thought I saw lovebirds. Thankfully, I was wrong."

"Do you have something against lovebirds?"

"Not anymore." One corner of her mouth lifted into a low-wattage smile. "Enjoy the remainder of your interview, Keith." With that, she moved away.

Keith's eyes roamed over every inch of Sadona's frame as she strolled away. "Good Lord, give me strength," he mumbled to himself.

Something was happening to him. She was the cause. He wasn't sure if he liked it. Wasn't sure if he disliked it. All he knew with any certainty was that it was too damn compelling to ignore. So, he wouldn't.

6

After scolding Buddy about his romp in the square that afternoon, Sadona had felt so guilty that she'd baked him a batch of dog-friendly peanut butter cookies and prepared doubled chocolate chip for herself. And for the past several hours, they'd snuggled together on the sofa and enjoyed their sweet treats.

Once her fourth Hallmark movie ended, she clicked the television off. Someone was finding their happily-ever-after—even if they were only fictional characters. "Well, at least I have you, boy," Sadona said, pulling at Buddy's ears.

She released a single laugh. Was this truly her new life? Had she really been reduced to spending her free time with a dog? Back in Atlanta, she'd enjoyed an active social life, things to do, friends to hang out with. Well, so-called friends who'd stopped taking her calls long ago. But should she have expected anything more? They'd been women married to Alec's friends. But still... Whatever happened to sister code?

Sadona blew a heavy breath, then ended her pity-party. *New beginnings*, she told herself. Everyone around her was living their lives; it was time she did a little living, too.

Without the distractions of the television, Keith popped into her head. She'd been so wrong that afternoon by assuming he'd been on a date. Learning it'd only been an interview had filled her with unexpected glee. Which was utterly ridiculous, because she wasn't interested in him. Well, not all that interested. *Curious*, she settled on. Yeah, that was it. She was just curious.

Rolling off the sofa, she headed into the kitchen to prepare dinner. Even though she was only cooking for one now, she still, on occasion, made elaborate meals. Tonight, she had a taste for cube steak smothered in gravy with onions and mushrooms, sautéed green beans, buttery mashed potatoes and rolls.

Over the past year, she'd gained almost twenty pounds. It had *mostly* landed in the right places, with the exception of the slight pudge at her stomach, affectionately known as her trouble region. For some odd reason, the extra weight made her feel liberated. Maybe because she was no longer under the watchful eye of her ex, who preferred her at *his* ideal weight.

The doorbell rang, startling Sadona from her thoughts. Buddy—her built-in visitor alert—stood at the door barking his cute little head off. While she wasn't expecting anyone, it wasn't unlike her sisters to pop in *to say hello* as they always put it. But she knew the real reason they occasionally dropped in was to check on her. Despite having families and lives of their own, they always, always were there for her. Not that she needed them to worry about her, she was grateful for their concern.

"Hush it, Buddy," Sadona said, washing her hands and heading to the door. "Coming."

Checking the peephole, she gasped and pulled away. A second later, she took another look to make sure her eyes weren't playing tricks on her. Nope, they weren't. It was Keith all right. In all of his sinfully chocolate glory. But what was he doing here?

"Um...one sec," she said, combing her fingers through her hair and ironing nonexistent wrinkles from the black tank top she wore. *Just curious*, she reminded herself before pulling the door open. "Keith. Hey."

"Hey. I know I should have called first. I hope I'm not disturbing you," he said.

"No worries. You're not disturbing me. Everything okay?"

"Yeah. Yeah, everything's fine. We were out for a run. Somehow I ended up on your doorstep. Figured I'd say hello. I hope that's okay."

Keith flashed a smile so beautifully brilliant, it snatched her breath away for a second or two. She thanked God for the wind that had blown Keith her way. "Absolutely." *Ugh, had that sounded too desperate?*

Sadona's eyes left Keith's and settled on the well-behaved chocolate Labrador Retriever seated at Keith's feet. The animal paid no attention to Buddy as he stepped onto the porch for a thorough inspection of their K9 visitor. Sadona bet he didn't force Keith to chase him through the square.

"And who is this?" she asked.

"This is Baxter. Say hello, Bax."

To Sadona's surprised, the dog lifted one of its large paws as if to shake her hand. The unexpected move startled Buddy. He gave a single bark, ran inside, stood behind her and peered around her leg. So much for being a fierce protector. All bark, no bite.

Sadona accepted the offered paw. "Hey, Baxter. Nice to meet you." Baxter didn't strike her as a dog that'd just gotten over a serious stomach bug—giving further weight to her suspicions—Keith had wanted her to fall in love with Buddy. Her gaze returned to his. Deciding to have a little fun with him, she said, "Baxter seems all better now. I guess this means you'll be taking Buddy tonight, right?"

The question appeared to baffle Keith for a second or two. Recovering, he said, "Um, yeah. Yeah. I mean, if you're sure."

Sadona rested a hand on her hip and narrowed her eyes. "You're not slick. Dr. Fremont. I know what you've been up to. You wanted me to fall in love with this dog, didn't you?"

He released a smooth, sexy chuckle. "Guilty. For the record, I'm not usually a dishonest person. But I suspected you really did want to keep him, just needed a little persuading. So did you? Fall in love with him, I mean."

She glanced at Buddy, still inspecting Baxter, but from a distance. "Between his gnawing on one of my favorite pair of shoes, chewing up an invoice and always hogging the sofa...yeah, I guess I kinda fell for him."

"Attracted to bad boys, huh?"

"Not usually. But this one...I just can't seem to resist."

"Lucky dog."

The comment staggered Sadona a moment. She scrutinized Keith to decipher if it had unintentionally slipped out. His confident expression told her it had been deliberate. If nothing else, the man was direct.

"So does that mean you're keeping him?"

"I'm keeping him. Who else would I bake peanut butter cookies for? Dog-friendly, of course," she added.

Baxter's ears perked, his head tilted and he made a noise that sounded strangely like *huh*.

Keith laughed. "You said the magic word." He lowered his tone, "Cookies."

She stepped aside. "Well, come inside so he can have one or two or three. However many he's allowed to have. I baked a ton."

"Free dog," Keith said.

Baxter stood and Keith led him through the door. Nope, Keith definitely didn't spend time chasing Baxter.

"He's well-trained, I see. I've been trying to teach Buddy to sit, but it's not sticking. That dog truly has a personality all his own."

They eyed Buddy and Baxter. Whereas Baxter

hadn't so much as glanced at Buddy before, he seemed mildly interested in him now. Particularly his muzzle. If she had to guess, Baxter smelled the peanut butter on Buddy's breath.

"Something smells delicious," Keith said, bending to remove Baxter's leash.

"I was in the middle of cooking dinner. Have you eaten?" she asked, then quaked at the question. Why was she being so ridiculous? There was nothing wrong with sharing an innocent meal with the man. They were friends—kinda, almost, close to being.

"Other than a granola bar before I left the clinic, no, I haven't."

"You're more than welcomed to stay. That's if you don't have other plans."

"I don't want to impose."

"Quit being ridiculous. As much as you've assisted me, I *owe* you a meal." She passed him the container of peanut butter cookies.

Popping off the top, he took a whiff. "*Mmm.* These smell delicious."

"Thank you. I found the recipe online."

Keith led Baxter back into the living room. Buddy followed like an obedient child, tossing scattered glances up at the container. With a finger, Keith made a downward motion, and Baxter lowered completely to the floor.

"Good boy," Keith said, then rewarded him with a cookie.

Stunned—again—by this dog and his owner

Sadona said, "You have got to teach me how to do that."

"To go down on all fours?"

Sadona swatted him playfully. "No, silly. How to make my wayward dog listen like Baxter does."

"It's all about consistency."

Keith gave Baxter another cookie, and he devoured it. When Buddy whined, perhaps wondering why he was being left out of the cookie loop, Keith knelt to his level.

"You have to ask your mommy. I don't want to get in trouble."

As if Buddy understood every word, he looked to Sadona. Who could resist those big, bright eyes? Using her finger as she addressed Buddy, she said, "One more. No more after that."

Buddy eagerly took the cookie from Keith's hand and gobbled it up.

"Baxter, stay," Keith said, then followed Sadona back into the kitchen.

Buddy stayed put, too. However, Sadona knew it had less to do with the command Keith had given Baxter and more to do with Buddy's search for crumbs.

Setting the container on the counter, Keith cupped his hands in front of himself, "Can I help with anything?"

"No. Just sit and relax."

"Come on, I have to do something. It wouldn't feel right to let you do all of the work."

His willingness to help was refreshing and

foreign. Could she ever remember a time when Alec had offered to help her prepare dinner? Then again, that had probably been for the best. Alec would have found something to complain about. "Okay, then. You can wash the beans."

"Perfect. I'm an excellent bean washer."

Sadona laughed. She liked the fact that Keith could so easily make her do that. Wait. No, she didn't. She didn't like it at all. And she didn't like him or his sense of humor, or the way her stomach fluttered when he gave her that lazy smile, or the way her body trembled slightly standing next to him.

An hour later, they sat down to dinner. Being a gentleman, he'd pulled out her chair, then pushed it in once she was seated. What really moved her was when he'd closed his hand over hers and said grace. Alec had never initiated the blessing. He'd always prompted her to do it. Not that she minded, she relished giving thanks, but to have the man of the house do it every now and then would have been great. Keith was like a breath of fresh air.

Another hour passed with Sadona and Keith talking, laughing, sharing comfortable beats of silence, then doing it all over again. One thing she'd quickly discovered about Keith...the man was not bashful when it came to eating. She couldn't help but snicker when he finished off another pile of mashed potatoes. Where did he put it all?

"What?" he asked.

"Nothing. I just enjoy watching you eat." Alec never savored her meals the way Keith had. "You have a big appetite. One never would guess by looking at you."

His body was a finely sculpted work of art. When she realized she'd been staring at the bulge at his bicep, she drew her attention away. Meeting his dark gaze, amusement twinkling in his eyes.

Busted.

Still, she couldn't help but wonder if he was as greedy in the bedroom. An image of his large hands cupping her breasts burned into her head. The tightening of her nipples forced her to drop-kick the tantalizing thought away.

"If you knew how long it has been since I've had a home-cooked meal this delicious, you'd feel sorry for me. And these mashed potatoes... I could eat the entire bowl."

He almost had. "Help yourself to fourths and fifths. If we run out, I'll make more."

"Do you always cook like this?"

"Not always. Some nights dinner is a bag of popcorn. But when I have a taste for something..." An elicit image of him filled her head. Forcing it away, she swiped her hand over the bounty of food, "...this happens."

A roguish grin flashed briefly on Keith's face, as if he'd been inside her head.

"I totally get having a taste for something. And I know those popcorn nights all too well. I'm not much of a cook, which means I'm constantly eating junk. Which is why I have to run. A lot."

"My sister's pregnant," she said. "It's also why I cook like this. She's been known to pop in for food. She gets *hangry* when she doesn't eat. She shamelessly blames the baby for her hunger anger."

They laughed.

"How far along is she?"

"Four and a half months. But if you ask her, she's twenty. In her defense, she does look like she's about to pop. I was convinced she was having twins until I saw the 3D ultrasound."

"Do twins run in your family?" Keith asked.

"Yes, on my father's side. My brother was a twin. Sadly, the other baby didn't survive childbirth."

Compassion spread across Keith's face.

"I'm sorry to hear that," he said.

"Thanks."

"So, you have a brother. Does he live here in Mount Pleasant, too?"

Sadona fingered the heart pendant dangling from the chain around her neck. Her brother Phoenix had given it to her what seemed like an eternity ago. She had to swallow her mounting emotion before she could speak. "He's deceased."

The expression on Keith's face suggested he regretted asking. Giving him—and herself—a reprieve, she said, "Do you have kids?"

Keith's gaze left her and sadness distorted his handsome features. "I had a son. KJ." A faint smile touched his lips, but melted away a millisecond later. "He was hit while playing in our cul-de-sac. A drunk driver. Our neighbor's seventeen-year-old-daughter. He was seven."

Her heart plummeted to her feet. Loss was never easy, but losing your child... She couldn't imagine and didn't want to. "Keith, I'm so, so sorry. I didn't mean to dredge up such a painful memory."

He raised a hand. "It was a long time ago."

By the pained expression on his face, the wound was still raw. How did anyone ever get over a tragedy like that? She felt an extreme amount of sympathy for him and an urge to drape her arms around him. She resisted.

Swallowing the lump of emotion stuck in her throat, she changed the subject to lighten the mood. "Did you save room for dessert?"

A lazy smile curled his lips. "I have been eyeing those chocolate chip cookies tucked away in the corner over there. My weakness."

"Ah. So Baxter got it honestly, huh?"

"Yes, he did."

They eyed Baxter across the room, still in the same spot Keith had left him. What was surprising, Buddy had claimed a spot next to him. Odd. Usually anytime food was in play, Buddy was right there giving her the please-give-me-just-a-nibble stare down.

Sadona chuckled. "I think Buddy has found a best friend."

"Looks that way. Guess this means we'll be spending quite a bit of time together. Play dates and such."

Though Keith flashed an innocent grin, something wicked shone in his eyes. Excitement heated her cheeks. "I guess so."

If her being in agreement shocked him, it didn't show on his face. They eyed one another in silence for a long while. Strangely, their connection felt as familiar as her favorite blanket—just as warm and cozy, too.

"Are you sure you're okay with that?" Keith asked, disturbing the silence.

Sadona quirked a brow. "Why wouldn't I be?"

When Keith's eyes lowered to her mouth, she had an idea of what was running through his head—their kiss—because it raced through hers, too. His gaze slowly returned, ushering in sexual tension that was so thick it made her lightheaded.

Or it simply could have been the fact that all the blood was rushing from her head and settling between her legs. "I better clean up these dishes and get those cookies." She stood and reached for his plate at the same time he reached for it. Their fingers grazed. "Ooo." Sadona yanked her hand back and rested it against her chest. "St-static electricity."

The electricity part was accurate, but static had nothing to do with it.

"I was thinking the same thing," he said.

Why didn't she believe him?

"Let me help you," Keith said.

When he made a motion to stand, Sadona stopped him by resting her hand on his solid shoulder. Huge mistake. The sensation that shot up her arm was like some dizzying elixir. Its effects were instant, potent, arousing and mystifying.

In movies, she'd seen where psychics touched a person and received visions of that person's past. But how was this touch-telepathy happening to her? This was real life, not some sci-fi flick. Plus, it wasn't the past she was seeing.

In her fantasy—daydream—vision—oh, hell, she wasn't sure what to call it—Keith shared her bed, their limbs tangled, mouths joined. These images were so life-like, she swore she could feel Keith's every touch, every swipe of his tongue.

When her system couldn't take any more, she pulled her hand away, balled it into a tight fist and rested it against her trembling belly. She stumbled back a step, the potency of the manifestation overstimulating her.

Keith stood, a look of uncertainty on his face. "Are you okay?"

No. No she wasn't. Clearly, she was losing her damn mind. However, she was determined to at least appear sane or as close to it as possible. "Yes, I'm fine. Sometimes when I stand too fast, I...um...get a little woozy." Okay, maybe that hadn't been the best explanation. When the concern lines crawling across Keith's forehead deepened, she was sure it hadn't been. "I'm fine."

She could see the wheels turning in Keith's head. The concern she witnessed on his face was genuine and tugged at her heart. Yes, she wanted to put his mind at ease, but there was no simple way to tell him her desire to make love to him had her manifesting wicked visions.

"Sit, Dr. Fremont. I promise you I'm okay."

After a couple of seconds of scrutiny, he lowered back into his seat. Walking away, Sadona smiled. It kinda felt good having someone other than her sisters worry about her—even if it had been in vain.

Sadona could feel Keith's eyes trailing her around the room. She wanted to believe he merely enjoyed looking at her, but it was more likely he thought she might drop dead at any minute.

"Okay, okay, okay. I lied," she blurted, unable to handle the guilt another second. "It wasn't standing too quickly that made me woozy. It was...you."

Keith's head jerked back in what she took to be surprise. Understandable.

"I see," was all he said before standing and closing the distance between them.

"Truth is..." She paused, debating whether or not to continue. Heck, she'd revealed this much, no use in hiding now. "The truth is I haven't stopped thinking about you since we kissed. I haven't really tried."

The corners of Keith's mouth twitched as though he were holding back a smile, pining to break free. She wished it would have blossomed. Maybe it would have loosened the knot in her belly.

As if her brain had been on a ten-second delay, it hit her. She'd really just confessed to not being able to stop thinking about him? *Oh God.*

For the record, she'd never had a problem expressing herself, but this was different. This was beyond a mere moment of expression. This was a confession of need, want, desire. As tempting as it was, she resisted asking him to forget everything she'd just said. As if he could have.

Silent, Keith folded his arms across his chest. The move tightened the olive green T-shirt across his chest, showing the outline of his pecs. Her brain stalled, and she instantly forgot how nervous she'd been just a moment ago. Her fingertips ached to touch him—anywhere, everywhere.

Bringing her gaze up to his caused her breath to hitch from the strict way he eyed her. "I've never done anything like this before," she said.

"Anything like what?" he said, finally breaking his silence.

Her tone was low when she said, "Sleep with a man I barely know."

7

Sadona noticed a slight shift in Keith's expression. She wasn't sure if it was confusion, appreciation, or excitement from the fact she was offering herself to him. Possibly a mix of all three. His scrutinizing stare wreaked havoc on her already overexerted system.

True, she wasn't an advocate for casual sex, but she was convinced if Keith didn't make love to her tonight she would die of sexual starvation. She was a big girl, she could handle one night of meaningless sex.

When Keith dropped back into silence again, she continued, "We're both adults. Don't worry, I'm not the stalker-type. I don't expect anything beyond tonight. We can go back to things as normal in—"

"I don't want to sleep with you, Sadona"

This time it was her head that snapped back in surprise. She pressed her brows together in confusion. Obviously, she'd read the situation all wrong. Was she that rusty when it came to men? Had she just shamelessly thrown herself at a man who didn't want her? Oh God, she was going to be sick.

Swallowing the bile burning the back of her throat, she said, "You don't?"

Keith rested a large hand on the side of her

neck, causing her to flinch. The electricity they produced could launch a rocket.

"You're not ready," he said.

Not ready? Not ready? Oh, he had no idea just how willing she was. Out of curiosity, she asked, "How do you know I'm not ready?" There was a little more snap in her words then she'd intended, but wasn't it justified after being rejected? Why did he think he knew what she was ready for? Just like a man to *assume*.

Keith brushed her cheek, causing her to flinch again. Damn him and all of his potent energy.

"If you were, you'd melt under my touch, not wince."

Wait. Did he think—

"You're uncomfortable with me, which is understandable. Call it a character flaw, but I'm greedy in the bedroom, Sadona. If we made love, I would want, *need*, all of you. Nothing held back."

Wanted and needed all of her? It may not have been the most appropriate reaction at the time, but Keith's words made her temperature rise, her heartbeat kick up a notch or two and caused her to tremble with desire. She wanted and needed all of him, too.

He backed away. "I'll help you clean up, then I'll get out of your hair."

Keith moved toward the table, but Sadona wasn't letting him get away so easily. The days of allowing things to go unsaid were over. "When I flinch, it's not because I don't want you, Keith

Fremont; it's because I do. Desperately." When Keith faced her again, his expression was unreadable. But she knew she had his full attention. "I haven't been with a man since my ex-husband. You...you evoke something inside me."

Keith came to stand directly in front of her. Clearly, he lived by the phrase: silence is golden, because he didn't utter a word. That was okay, because there was more she needed to say.

"I've never experienced sparks when my ex touched me. Never. But when you touch me, it's like an explosion goes off inside of me. It's beautiful and scary all at the same time. I can't explain why it's you who causes it, but you do. It's not flinches or winces you feel when you touch me, Keith; it's aftershocks."

Sadona exhaled, not believing she'd just said all of that. She was becoming Rana, the more verbally-unconstrained of the three sisters. However, expressing herself this way felt...*fantastic*. She'd grown accustomed to censoring herself to appease Alec. No more. This was a new day; she was a new woman.

"And you're wrong about something else," she said.

Keith's eyes narrowed on her. "And what's that?"

"I am comfortable with you. So comfortable it's a bit off-putting. You feel like an old friend I've known all my life. Maybe I should have kept my longing to myself, but I'm done with leaving things unsaid. I apologize if I've made things uncomfortable for you. And I truly understand if you need to put some distance between us. But I hope we can be friends, because I really do like you. As a person. Not just as a penis."

Sweet Jesus, had she really just said that? Oh God, she had.

Redirecting her focus away from Keith, she moved to the sink, turned on the water and waited for the basin to fill. This would give him an opportunity to escape and her the chance to put several feet in her mouth.

Not just as a penis. Really, Sadona?

A warm sensation crawled up her spine. She didn't need to turn to know Keith stood directly behind her. He reached around and shut off the water. His warm chest nestled against her back and his hands rested on either side of the counter, pinning her in place.

Sadona closed her eyes and relished the feel of his hard frame pressed up against her. She pulled in a deep breath, then released it slowly. The move did absolutely nothing to steady her erratic pulse rate, her thudding heartbeat, or her shaky nerves.

When Keith's soft, gentle lips pressed a kiss to the crook of her neck, she gasped from the extreme exhilaration. He kissed her again—this time on the side of the neck—then once more below her lobe. Her nipples beaded inside her bra and wetness pooled between her legs.

She wanted him like she'd never wanted anyone in her life. But of course there had to be complications. Keith's words were warm, steady, and low against her ear when he spoke.

"Not too long ago you said you were still picking up pieces. What changed?

"My perspective," she said, barely able to think straight under his delicious torture.

"Explain that to me, Sadona."

Keith's mouth moved to the opposite side. Inching the strip of fabric down, he peppered kisses to her shoulder.

"I..." She moaned. "How do you expect me to focus when you're doing...that?"

"I can stop."

"No." The urgency of the word startled her. "Don't." She tilted her head to the side to allow him better access.

Why had her perspective changed? It could have been because of the news she'd received from Alec earlier that day. It could have been the ping of unease she'd felt seeing Keith with another woman. It could have been simply because she wanted him. It could have been a mix of all three, or none at all.

"To answer your question, I no longer believe I need to have all the pieces in place before I can start living my life again. I know it sounds like I expect more, but I'm not asking for a commitment from you, Keith. I don't want to disturb your bachelor lifestyle," she said for comic relief.

84

Without warning and against her protest, Keith stopped. A second later, he turned her to face him. Their gazes held for a short time.

"I have really tough hands," he said.

Sadona hadn't really understood the comment, but assumed he was merely interjecting his own humor into the conversation. "Well, I'm sure one of my products can help with that."

Keith shook his head. "Nah. If my hands are all soft and tender, how will I help you pick up the sharp pieces? That's if you want my help."

Unshed tears of sentiment stung her eyes. *This man.*

The idea of a relationship scared the hell out of her, but the notion of being with Keith caused a soothing effect. "Tough is good," she said.

Keith cradled her face and stared into her eyes. Though she may have been a little rusty when it came to the opposite sex, she wasn't blind. What she saw in Keith's probing gaze was pure and raw desire. He wanted her. She was sure of it. But something else lingered there, as well.

"This is what I want, Keith," she said, answering the unasked question his silence posed. "But if you're uncertain about giving it to me, I under—"

His mouth covered hers, capturing the remainder of her sentence. She froze from the unexpected move, but their connection soon thawed her. The kiss was everything. Hungry. Intensely satisfying. Perfect. Even better than the first, which was a bit staggering since she hadn't believed it could get any better than that. She didn't regret being wrong.

Keith hoisted her up and onto the counter, never skipping a tantalizing beat. He continued to feast on her mouth as though it were a meal he'd craved for centuries and had finally received. But not only did he feast, he also fed. Nourished every starving inch of her ultra-aroused body. And his bounty of pleasure was five-star delicious.

Sadona attributed this ravenous need for Keith to the fact it had been a long time since she'd been in the throes of passion. But it felt like much more. Like he was a necessary route along her journey of rediscovery.

The intensity of the kiss lessened, becoming slow and gentle. Still, her body ached out of control for him. When he inched her closer to the edge of the counter, his erection pressed against her throbbing core. The unexpected delight snatched her breath away.

Tearing her mouth from his, she said, "Down the hall, to the left."

When Keith slid her off the counter, she instinctively wrapped her legs around him. They kissed all the way to her bedroom. It was a miracle he hadn't dropped her as they fumbled down the hall.

Buddy beat them to the bed, jumping in and snuggling into his spot.

Keith lowered Sadona to her feet, then lifted

the dog. "Not tonight, boy. Tonight, your mommy's all mine." He placed Buddy outside the room and closed the door.

Buddy whined once or twice, then went silent. A second later, his claws tapped down the hallway.

Sadona liked the idea of being all Keith's tonight. Probably too much. What would she be beyond their night together? What did she want to be? Her head-chatter ended the second Keith removed his shirt, his sculpted torso garnering all of her attention.

Before she'd even realized it, her hands had come up to explore. This was definitely not the mid-section of an admitted junk-food lover. With the tip of her index finger, she followed the line of fine black hairs until it disappeared below the waistband of his jeans. Meeting Keith's gaze, she shivered from the amount of lust-laden desire she saw in his eyes. He walked her back until her legs bumped against the mattress.

"Do you know how many times I've fantasized about this moment? Dreamed about undressing you? Languished on the many things I'd do to your naked body?" he said.

Sadona swallowed hard. "No," she said, despite being fairly certain he hadn't been in search of an answer.

"Plenty. To the point of near insanity."

When he flashed a sexy grin, it compounded her need to be with him. She considered asking him to tell her the things he'd envisioned, but had a better idea. "Show me," she said. "That's if you're up for it."

It had been a blatant challenge, one that Keith appeared eager to accept. He undressed her, leaving her maroon bra and panty set in place. He took a step back and allowed his eyes to roam over her body. Self-conscious about the small swell at her mid-section, she crossed a hand in front of her.

Keith shook his head. "I want you full-strength, never watered down."

"Yes, daddy" played on the tip of her tongue, but instead of allowing it to escape, she only nodded.

He peeled her hand away. "Woman, let this be the last time you ever try to hide any part of your body from me."

"Okay." She sounded like a once-taunted child whose father had just convinced her of how beautiful she truly was. It stuck.

His hungry eyes raked over her again. Her eyes went on a journey of their own. As if she were watching someone pump air into a balloon, Keith's erection grew and grew, pushing against the fabric of his jeans and causing her to bite down hard on her bottom lip.

Whatever move he intended to make, she prayed he hurried up and make it, because she desperately needed a release. A second later, he moved to the bed and eased down, leaving her standing in the floor.

He held out his hand. "Come here."

Taking it, he directed her between his legs. His large hands rested on her hips. When he dipped forward and placed a kiss on her stomach, she trembled. How in the hell had such a simple action caused such a reaction?

After several more kisses to her trouble region, Keith's hands glided up her body—slow and steady. He removed her bra in one skillful motion, bringing relief to her aching nipples.

"Beautiful," he said. He cupped her breasts in his hands and smoothed his thumbs over her budded nubs. "Perfect."

With the tip of his tongue, he circled her areola, then sucked a taut nipple into his mouth. Sadona cried out from the instant sensations that sparked through her entire body. Keith feasted on her—licking, flicking, twirling his tongue. Sucking, pulling, teasing her with his lips.

Then, he did the exact same thing to the opposite breast, leaving her woozy. If this were the type reaction she had to him satisfying her breasts, what would happen when he pleasured the rest of her? Pure delirium, she concluded.

Supremely aroused, the next several minutes were a blur—Keith standing, maneuvering her onto the bed, undressing himself. Joining her on the bed, he rested at her feet and on his knees. Her eyes blazed a fiery line down his torso, over his tongue-worthy pecs, along his ripped midsection, beyond the curling black hairs, settling on the most impressive erection she'd ever seen anywhere other than television.

Sadona's jaw went slack. "You're...it's...noteworthy," she said, doubting it was the first time he'd heard such a thing.

Keith flashed a half smile, dripping with mischief. "I'm glad you think so."

His expression turned stern, and he eyed her with a hungry, heat-filled, assessing stare.

"What is it?" she asked.

A second or two passed before he spoke. "I'm going to give your body what I think it needs, Sadona. Afterwards, you can tell me what it wants—especially if I haven't satisfied you adequately enough."

Oh, she had no doubt he'd satisfy her divinely without her input. Still, his concern for her fulfillment was refreshing. "Okay."

Lifting her left leg, he placed a kiss to the arch of her foot, then ankle, calf and lastly, her inner thigh. Her breathing grew heavy and shallow as he peppered kisses higher and higher. And when his soft, wet, warm lips touched her core, she clenched fistfuls of the sheet between her fingers and cried out in a long, throaty moan.

He kissed her swollen lips once, twice, and a third time for good measure, she assumed. With a stiff tongue, he parted her folds and circled her clit several times before suckling her.

"Oh...my—" Her words seized in her throat, the pre-sizzle of an orgasm crawling up her spine. *Too soon*, she warned her capsizing body. The warning had been in vain. There was no recovering from the swell threatening to engulf her.

Keith's hands gripped her thighs, as if to make sure she didn't get away from him, then buried his face even deeper between her legs. The sheer amount of pleasure derived from what he did with his skillful tongue couldn't be put into words, but the sounds she emitted had to be a pretty good indication of how much she enjoyed it.

Buddy barked on the opposite side of the door—probably thinking she was in distress. His protest distracted her from the heat pooling in her belly, the tingling in her limbs, the flame igniting at her center. Unfortunately, it wasn't enough to ward off the release.

"Keith," she screamed, her back arching off the bed, then collapsing back down as though she'd lost control of her body. And in a way, she had. The orgasm slammed into her so intensely that for several moments, not a single one of her five senses functioned properly.

Her sight was the first to filter back with the first thing she saw being Keith's handsome face. His lips moved, but it only translated into a serious of hums. "What? I can't—"

His mouth crashed down on hers, his greedy kiss swallowing her words. They kissed for what felt like a lifetime, their link recharging her body. When Keith finally pulled away, her breathing was erratic, and so was his.

"Wha...what did you say?" she asked, the

buzzing in her ears finally subsiding.

Keith kissed the corner of her mouth. "I said, I want you to give it all to me tonight. No holding back."

Sadona moaned when he dragged his tongue along the column of her neck, then nipped her skin. "It's been a long time for me. I have a whole lot to give. Are you sure you can handle it?"

Keith's head rose and his eyes settled on her. The gleam in his dark gaze told her there was absolutely no doubt in his mind that he could.

He reached over and removed the condom he'd, at some point, placed on the nightstand. God, she prayed he had more than just that one. If she didn't know anything else, she knew only making love once with this man would not be enough.

After Keith sheathed his shaft, he positioned himself between her legs. Like with everything he'd done up to this point, he took his time entering her. Holding his dick in his hand, he teased her sensitive clit, then dipped just the tip inside her.

Her opening stretched to accommodate his girth. But there was no pain, just unbridled pleasure and a need for more. Pulling out, Keith slid the tip in again, giving her a couple more inches this time.

"*Keith*. Don't make me beg," she said. "Give it to me."

He gripped her hips and drove himself all the way inside her. A screech escaped past her lips and he cursed under his breath. With slow, smooth, steady strokes, Keith forced her body under his control. Her hips clumsily rocked back and forth. Soon, they fell into a sweet harmony meeting each other's thrusts at just the right time and just the right angle.

Keith's hands glided up her ribcage and cupped her breasts. Using his thumbs, he teased her sensitive nipples. A second later, he dipped forward and pulled one of the taut buds between his lips and rolled the other between his fingers.

He kissed his way to her mouth and covered it with his. Their tongues sparred in a delicious battle of wills. If he'd been affixed with a warning label, it would have read: EXTREMELY ADDICTIVE.

Keith placed a hand behind one thigh and pushed her leg toward her chest, then drove himself even deeper inside her. *Oh no*, she thought as the familiar sensation swirled in her belly. *No, no, no*. She didn't want it to end. Not yet. It felt too damn good. Unfortunately, that was the problem.

Whimpering against his mouth, she dug her nails into his damp flesh as another powerful orgasm took full hold of her. Her entire body responded to the lightning bolts of satisfaction sparking through her. The inner muscles of her core pulsed and clenched around him. He grunted a string of chest-rumbling sounds. A beat later, he came, intensifying her release.

Keith fell onto his back, then pulled her spent body against him. Earlier, she hadn't been convinced once would be enough. But she was sure she couldn't handle another round just yet, so this was nice.

"Now," Keith started in a heavy breath, "tell me what your body wants."

Sadona placed a kiss under his chin. "You've already given it to me and then some."

Keith playfully pinched her butt cheek, and she could hear the smile in his voice when he spoke again.

"Pleasing you had been my mission."

Sadona snuggled even closer against him and closed her heavy eyes. She loved the feel of his body, hard and warm. Yeah, she could definitely get used to this. Kissing him again, she said, "Mission accomplished, Dr. Fremont. Mission accomplished."

Soothing silence filled the room. She'd forgotten just how great it felt to be held, to feel protected. No, one night of this wouldn't be enough. Her body would require more of this, more of Keith. Shouldn't that scare her?

Keith's voice brought her back to reality before she could give her question any more thought, before fear, doubt and the past tainted this moment.

"What were you wondering?" Keith asked.

"Wondering?"

"Your voicemail message. You said you were wondering and then you disconnected the call."

Ah, the message she'd been making right before spotting Keith through the bakery window.

"Oh. I was calling to see if you wanted to have coffee or something."

"Yes. Especially the *or something*."

"You can have as much of the *or something* you'd like."

8

Although Sadona had talked to Keith a couple of hours prior, she felt an overwhelming need to call him at that moment. So, she did. The second he answered, she knew something was off by his weary tone. Plus, he usually responded with some silly greeting like: "You couldn't go another second without hearing my voice, huh?" This time he'd simply given a drab "Hello."

"Hey," she said. "Everything okay?"

"Hey. Yeah." He sighed. "I had to euthanize a dog a little while ago."

Sadona's heart instantly went out to Keith and the dog's owner. She couldn't imagine having to put Buddy to sleep. In the short time she'd had him, the dog had dug a special place in her heart. Though she knew he wouldn't live forever, she didn't even want to think about losing him. "I'm sorry. I can imagine how hard that must have been for you."

"It's the least favorite part of my job. But it was necessary. He had cancer and had been suffering."

"Are you okay?"

"It's strange. Despite the number of times I've had to do this over the years, it always has an effect on me."

Sadona imagined that it would. "You're

probably a deep feeler. You experience the world through emotions, which can cause strong responses to things like this. Deep feelers can be highly sensitive and have strong emotional responses. It's natural, though."

Keith chuckled. "Okay. That's quite an insightful explanation. How much do I owe you, Dr. Lassiter?"

Sadona laughed, liking that Keith's tone sounded more upbeat than it had moments ago. She wasn't sure why the idea of him being sad bothered her so much, but it did. Could it have been because she was really feeling him? *No*, she told herself. They were just no-stringing it. There were no emotions allowed.

Why had she felt such a strong need to phone him? Maybe it was the aural energy they exchanged each time they made love. And a lot of energy had been swopped. They'd slept together almost every night for the past three weeks. She'd read that the more two people interacted intimately, the deeper the connection they had to one another.

Kicking the radical thoughts racing around in her head aside, she said, "Sorry. I've read a lot of mind, body, soul and psychology books over the past year."

"Ah," was all he said.

"So, am I right? Are you a deep feeler, Dr. Fremont?"

"Well, you'll just have to judge that for

yourself, *Ms*. Lassiter."

Of course most men wouldn't admit to being sensitive, and Keith was no exceptions. If she had to guess, he wore his heart on his shelve. Thinking back to the passionate speech he'd given about black men looking for their queens, she could almost guarantee it. "I like a good mystery," she said.

They chatted a little while longer about nothing in particular.

"Your call has perked me up, but I believe seeing your gorgeous face would have an even greater effect. How about lunch? I've wanted to try that new pizza place on Main," Keith said.

"I wish I could, but I have to work through lunch. I'm swamped." Which wasn't entirely a lie. Carolina Lavender had taken off overnight. Thanks to Rana having her mother-in-law spread the word to some of her wealthy friends.

"Oh. Okay," Keith said. "Gotta do whatcha gotta do."

Hearing something in his tone, Sadona felt the need to add further explanation. "Gadiya was helping, but after about an hour, she needed a nap." The last time she'd checked, Gadiya was knocked out on one end of the sofa and Buddy on the other. "Good help is so hard to find."

She chuckled but Keith remained uncomfortably quiet. Something was wrong, but what?

"How about dinner?" he asked.

Sadona smiled. "Dinner, I can do."

"Great. I'll pick you up around six. The—"

Sadona cut him off mid-thought. "I have a better idea. How about you pick up Chinese and we eat in. Afterward, we can get creative with dessert."

A beat or two of silence played between them before Keith gave a dry, "Huh."

Huh. That definitely meant something. "Should I ask?" she said.

Keith sighed. "Maybe I am a deep feeler, Sadona, because I'm starting to believe you don't want to be seen in public with me. My feelings are a little hurt."

Sadona massaged the side of her neck, doing the first thing that came to mind. Deflecting. "What? That's ridiculous, Keith." But knowing he wasn't too far from the truth.

"Is it?"

"Of course it is." And the fact that he would say it angered her. Or maybe it was the fact that he'd called her out—stepped on her toes, as her grandmother used to put it—that angered her.

"Every time I've suggested we go out someplace—the movies, bowling, dinner—there's always a reason why you can't go: work, Buddy, your sisters. We've never even gone on a first date, Sadona."

"Why do we need to parade around town? Why do we need a first date? It's not like we're in a committed relationship, Keith. We're just screwing."

Sadona instantly regretted her tone and the cold thing she'd just said. It never failed, whenever she felt cornered, she lashed out. Keith had definitely boxed her in. Closing her eyes, she kneaded the tension ache in her shoulder. "I didn't—"

"Yep, definitely a deep feeler," Keith said, cutting her off. "I owe you an apology, Sadona, because I assumed—" He stopped. "Damn. There I go assuming again."

Sadona ignored his sarcasm. Mainly because it had been warranted. Had she been the one on the receiving end, she would have been hurt, too. "Keith—"

"I have to go, Sadona. I have patients waiting."

"I'm afraid," she blurted. "That's why I keep making up excuses. I'm afraid."

Silence lingered on the opposite end and for a second, she thought Keith had disconnected. A feeling of relief settled over her when he spoke.

"Afraid of what?" he said.

"Falling for you, a relationship, trusting again, whether I'm enough, how—"

"Whether you're enough," Keith said.

The idea of revealing so much to Keith was unnerving. For so long, she'd kept so much to herself. Having someone to share it with was refreshing, but also scary, because it made her vulnerable. "Yes. My ex had an affair. Obviously, I wasn't—"

"Stop right there, Sadona. There could have been a hundred reasons why your ex-husband *chose* to have an affair and not a single one could have had anything to do with you."

Keith was right, but still, the idea stayed lodged in the back of her head. Wasn't it a thought that every woman who's been cheated on had? Surely, she wasn't the only one.

"I want to get to know you, Sadona. We can take things as slowly as you need to go. But I want to get to know you. Not just sexually. Let's just flow with this current and see where it takes us?"

He sounded like Rana. They weren't committing, but they weren't walking away from each other, either. What was the harm in exploring this? Nothing, she quickly determined. "Okay."

***

When Sadona had told Keith she had the perfect first date planned for them, he'd thought a movie, followed by dinner, possibly a walk in the park and a night of unbridled passion. Painting her workshop had never crossed his mind. Yet, here he stood in his damn underwear—because he'd dressed for a night out on the town—bedazzling one wall with glitter paint.

Sadona glanced over at him and smiled. "Best first date ever, right?" Her eyes performed a slow descent down his body. "I can't wait for the goodnight kiss."

When she pulled her bottom lip between her teeth, he playfully covered himself with his hand. "Excuse me. Could you please stop eyeing me like a piece of meat? I'm trying to work here."

Keith made the mistake of allowing his eyes to travel beyond her face, over the white tank she wore, then continue to her smooth, brown thighs. When she'd told him to remove his clothes, so he wouldn't soil them with paint, he'd pled his case that if he had to be in his underwear than so should she. She'd agreed—to a degree.

Though he hadn't been able to convince her to remove her shirt, she had sacrificed her bra. His eyes rose to her breasts, and his mouth watered at the sight of her taut nipples. They hadn't been that way just a moment ago. He stirred below the waist. The daydream of lowering her to the floor and burying himself deep inside her was interrupted by Sadona clearing her throat.

"Ahem."

His gaze rose and met her narrow-eyed scrutiny. Playing oblivious, he said, "What?"

"I do recall you saying you were trying to work. Don't let me distract you. We're almost done." She neared him, trailing a finger down his chest and hooking it inside his underwear. "And when we're done..." She bounced her brows twice leaving the rest unsaid.

Pretending to be appalled, he removed her hand and took a step back. "I'm not sure what type of man you think I am, Ms. Lassiter, but I don't sleep with women on the first date."

Sadona burst out laughing and so did he. Probably because they both knew good and well that all she had to do was blow on him and his dick would get hard. This woman should not have that much control over him or his body, but she did.

An hour later, Keith performed the last stroke of the second coat. When they'd first started, he'd had his doubts about Sadona's sparkly vision. But now, seeing it completed, he had to admit the wall tied in nicely with the one chalkboard wall and two dark grey ones, as well as the room's purple color scheme.

Sadona rushed back into the room. She'd taken a call from her sister nearly thirty minutes ago. Judging by the expression on her face, it had drained her.

"I'm so sorry about that. Gadiya was having another pregnancy-induced breakdown."

"Everything okay?"

She massaged her temple. "Yes. She was in love with the color of the nursery this morning. Tonight, she hates it and wants to repaint it for the fourth time. Poor Nico."

Keith wrapped Sadona in his arms. "You're not going to wake up in the middle of the night and decide you want to repaint this wall, are you?"

"I'm not pregnant, so I think you're safe."

An image of Sadona's belly swollen with his child burned into his head. The vision should have rattled him, but it didn't. Did she want kids? She'd been married, but had never had them. Maybe she didn't want kids. Would he be okay with it if she didn't?

Keith laughed at himself. Why was he even thinking about any of this? They were far from the I-want-you-to-have-my-baby stage. Hell, they hadn't even declared they were in a relationship. Plus, they were always protected against any accidents.

"What are you thinking about?"

Sadona's sweet voice cut into his thoughts. Stealing a peck, he said, "Compensation. For all of the hard work I've put in."

"I'm not a rich woman, but I'm sure I can provide at least one thing of value that can satisfy you—your bill, I meant to say," she corrected with a smirk. "But I'd be remised to pay for a job not yet complete."

Confused, Keith arched a brow. "What does that mean?" He hoped she didn't have any more walls needing to be painted.

"It means…" Her warm hand snaked into his underwear and wrapped around his dick, causing it to throb even more. "…I have one more critical task for you."

Sadona pumped him slowing, and Keith swore he was going to explode right then and there. "And what's that," he asked in a shaky voice.

She lowered to her knees and inched his underwear down. "Enjoy what I'm about to do to you. And once you've recovered, we can go out."

The second Sadona captured him inside her warm, wet mouth, his knees nearly buckled. "Oh, yes." Closing his eyes, he allowed his head to recline back as a gazillion sensations zapped through his entire body. Tangling his fingers in her hair, he brought his head up and watched her take him in and out of her mouth.

Something told him they wouldn't be making it out. And that was all right with him.

9

Over the past month and a half, Sadona had spent almost every night in Keith's arms. Regardless of how much they made love, he just couldn't get enough of her. He'd had sex plenty over the past several years, but no woman had ever come close to satisfying him in the way this woman had. Ever.

He sat on the edge of the bed and watched her sleep. His eyes roamed the length of her partially-covered body, appreciating every delicate inch. Washing a hand over his head, he blew a heavy breath. He was a goner. Actually, that realization had come the very first time she'd fallen asleep in his arms, but he was only now comfortable with admitting it.

There was no doubt in his mind that she belonged in them. The idea of any other man ever touching, kissing, pleasing Sadona in the ways he had, made his blood boil. Maybe she was unsure about what she wanted, but he wasn't. He wanted her.

Leaning forward, he placed several kisses on her exposed shoulder. "Wake up, sleeping beauty."

Sadona squirmed, cracked one eye and smiled. "What are you doing up?"

"I have to go."

"Go? *Noooo*," she said in a pouty tone. "It can't be morning already."

He laughed because they went through the same routine every time. "I would love to stay in bed with you all day, but I have to go home and get ready for work."

She poked out her bottom lip. "Sad face. What time is it?"

He glanced at his watch. "A little past six-thirty."

"Six-thirty?" she said as if she couldn't believe it. "I slept through the night?"

The idea seemed to astonish her. She had mentioned that she rarely got a full night's sleep. But he had yet to witness even one sleepless night. "You didn't budge a muscle all night long. Not even when I eased out of bed. I put it on you. Go 'head and admit it."

Sadona tried unsuccessfully to stifle a smile. Rolling her eyes heavenward, she said, "You were all right, I guess. I'll need many more experiences to fully make an accurate assessment of your performance, Dr. Fremont."

"I feel pretty confident that I can make that happen."

When he leaned in to give her a kiss on the lips, she stopped him.

"I have morning breath," she said, covering her mouth.

"Woman, if you don't give your man a kiss, I'm…" His words trailed after noticing the perplexed expression on her face. "What?" he asked, despite having a good idea of what had spooked her. They hadn't classified what they were doing as a 'relationship,' but that's precisely what it was, which meant it was time to add the label. She wasn't going anywhere and he wasn't either.

Sadona inched up in the bed, rested her back against the headboard and covered herself with the blanket as if she hadn't wanted him to see her nude body. Obviously, she hadn't considered the fact that he'd spent most of the night exploring her with his tongue. Too late for bashfulness now.

"Talk to me. What's wrong?" he said.

Her eyes lowered. Regardless of what her coyness suggested, he knew she felt a little something for him. And he felt a lot of something for her. He didn't want to scare her off, but he didn't want to continue to feel as if he were blowing aimlessly in the wind, either. It was time to define things.

"One mistake I made in my marriage was sacrificing myself and sometimes my happiness for the sake of my ex. To make him feel whole, I often avoided sharing my true thoughts and opinions, slowly chipping away pieces of who I really was. I will *never* be that woman again, Keith. Can you handle that?"

Keith inched closer to her. "Listen to me and hear me well. I don't ever want you to be anyone other than who you truly are, Sadona Lassiter. I always want you to be unapologetically you. Full-strength, never watered down."

Sadona eyed him for a moment. "I've heard

you can judge the heart of a man by the way he treats animals. If that's true, your heart is platinum. I could use someone like you in my life."

"So, does that mean you want me to be your man?"

Her lips curled into a smile. "Yes, Keith Fremont, I guess I want you as my man."

Good, but not enough. He shook his head. "Nah, sugar lips. I need you to *know* you want me as your man."

If she'd had a problem with the pet name he'd just given her, she didn't voice it. Instead, she smiled and nodded.

"I want you as my man."

"Are you sure you don't want to take a minute or two to think about it? This is a big step for you."

For them both, if he were being honest. He'd never imagined ever feeling this way about anyone—especially after such a short time—but Sadona was like a spell that couldn't be broken by a mere mortal like himself, so what was the use in trying? Especially when he didn't want to be free.

"I'm more than sure."

"I get it. You don't want any other woman's hands on all of this." He scanned his hands over his body. "Go ahead and admit it."

Sadona smirked. "That, too. But mainly because there's something special about you, Dr. Fremont. I can feel it."

He lifted her hand to his mouth and kissed her palm. "Does that mean your man gets a kiss?"

"How can I resist. But..." she peeled back the covers, hopped out of bed and dashed into the bathroom, "give me two seconds."

Watching her ass jiggle as she moved across the floor stirred something inside him, causing him to instantly crave her. Damn, he had it bad.

Several minutes later, she returned with minty fresh breath. Still naked, she stood between his legs and dipped her mouth to his. Securing his arms around her waist, he lowered onto the mattress.

Sadona's sweet tongue sparred with his. Desire flooded his loins, and his erection pressed against his zipper, demanding to be freed and relieved. His hands crawled along her ribcage and to her butt, giving it a firm squeeze.

"Mmm. I want you," she said, dragging her tongue across his bottom lip.

In one swift motion, he had her on her back. "You've got me." In more ways than she knew.

"All to myself?"

Keith stared deep into her eyes. "I'm all yours, baby. Every inch of me," he said, lowering his mouth to hers and starting something that had to be finished before he could leave.

***

By the time Keith made it into the office, he was almost twenty minutes late for his first appointment. "I know, I know," he said to a hand-on-hips Adda, lingering at his office door.

"You're never late," she said, moving farther into the room and eyeing him suspiciously.

"Baxter..." He thought twice about shamelessly implicating his dog in his tardiness. And he definitely couldn't tell her he was late because he'd been balls deep inside of Sadona. Though, Adda would have probably loved to hear that he was actually getting some on the regular. "I was up late. Working. Hard," he added with hidden innuendo.

Adda studied him thoroughly, tilting her head from one side to the other.

"What?"

"Something about you has been different for the past few weeks. Smiling nonstop. Gotta little more pep in your step. Chest all swollen with confidence. *Mmm-hmm.* Something was hard all right. Did you use protection?"

"Of course, I—" He stopped abruptly, realizing he'd stepped right into the scheming woman's trap.

Adda smirked. "I knew it was just a matter of time for you two. The chemistry had been potent enough to set the entire building on fire."

"I didn't mention a name," Keith said.

"You didn't have to."

Adda headed toward the door, but stopped before exiting. "By the way, she looks damn good on you."

Yeah, she felt damn good on him, too. But he kept that to himself.

Thankfully, the day zipped by, and by five o'clock, Keith was dog tired. All he wanted to do was go home, drop face first onto the mattress and sleep several hours.

Baxter greeted him the second he entered the house. "What's up, boy. Did you miss me?"

Baxter barked several times.

"I missed you, too."

When his cell phone rang, he fished it from his pocket. Craven's name lit the screen. Putting him on speaker, Keith moved toward his bedroom. "What's up?"

"You, man. You didn't forget about me, did you?"

"Forget—" *Shit*. He did. "I'll be there in fifteen minutes."

"Thanks, man. I owe you."

Craven had given up his bachelor pad and moved back home to take care of his father who'd been diagnosed with stage two Parkinson's disease. Keith commended and admired his friend's dedication to Daddy Monroe. Craven had a lot on his plate—caregiver to an ailing parent, running a business and going to school at night to get his business degree. Every now and then, Keith sat with Daddy Monroe when needed.

"No, you don't. I got your back."

After a quick shower, Keith and Baxter headed out the door. On the drive over, he called Sadona and told her he was helping out a friend and would stop by to tuck her in and kiss her goodnight on his way home, if it wasn't too late. Admittedly, he liked the idea of having someone to share his plans with.

Sadona had called him a good man for helping out a friend. He'd appreciated and accepted the compliment, along with the air kisses she sent over the line. They chatted until Keith arrived at the all-brick Victorian-style home. On request, he sent an air kiss or two of his own. Ending the call, he shook his head and laughed at himself. "Baxter, what is this woman doing to me?"

Exiting the vehicle, Baxter beat him to the front door, then darted past Craven when the door opened.

"Well, hello to you, too, Baxter," Craven said, some kind of pastry dangling from his mouth.

"Get out of here before you're late," Keith said.

"You know where everything is. I should be back no later than 9:30. There's plenty of food in the kitchen. Thank you again for this. You're a lifesaver. Pray I ace this test. Love you, Pop," he called out. "I'll see you a little later."

"Okay, son. Love you, too," came from the other room.

They fist bumped and Craven was out.

Keith entered the living room and shook his head. Baxter had already taken his place on the couch, his head in Daddy Monroe's lap. Daddy Monroe loved visits from Baxter and Baxter loved visiting him. Keith suspected it was because the man rubbed Baxter nonstop.

Keith noticed the shaking in Daddy Monroe's hands was worse than usual, but it didn't seem to interfere with his task. "What's up, Daddy Monroe? You good?"

"Doing fine, young head. Lord saw fit for me to see another day. How you?"

Daddy Monroe's speech was slurred, but Keith understood him just fine. "Fantastic," Keith said, easing down.

"You're awfully chipper. What's her name?"

Keith laughed. "Come on. Why does a woman have to be involved?"

"I might be old and shaky, but I'm not senile. Only a woman can make a man feel *fantastic*. And not just any woman. My Colleen, God rest her soul, made me feel fantastic for over three decades. When you find a woman you want to spend decades with, not just one night, you know you gotcha something good."

Keith couldn't swear he was at the decade's stage, but he did feel as if he had him something good. "Sadona," he said. "That's her name."

"Sadona. That's a pretty name. Treat her right."

He would, because he knew how it felt to be treated wrong.

Daddy Monroe continued, "Love her if you can. But if you can't, let her go so she can find someone who will."

"You're just full of wisdom tonight, huh?"

"I have my moments."

Keith wasn't sure when it happened, but somewhere between the wisdom and him closing his eyes for just a second, he'd dozed off. Gentle slaps on the side of his face drew him from the best dream of his life. Sadona was doing unbelievable things with her mouth and a damn grapefruit.

"Wake up, sleeping beauty."

Craven's voice filtered into his head. Keith opened his eyes to see the brown-skinned man standing over him.

"What—or who—are you dreaming about that's got you moaning and groaning like that?"

"*Sadona*," Daddy Monroe said. "That's his boo-thang."

Craven's brows bunched. "Sadona...*Lassiter*?"

A knot tightened in the pit of Keith's stomach. The first thought to flood his head was that the notorious playboy had slept with Sadona. *His* Sadona. That would change everything.

***

The frantic ringing of the doorbell caused Sadona to jolt, then smile. *Keith*. He'd said he might stop by if it wasn't too late. *10:30*. Perfect timing. 'Course, no time would have been too late in her opinion.

When she opened the door, something about the unreadable expression on Keith's face gave her pause. "Hey," she said. "You...okay?"

Keith cradled her face and crushed his mouth

to hers and kissed her in that all-consuming manner he did each time their lips touched. Too greedy to pull away for an explanation, she simply enjoyed what he was doing to her mouth, body and soul. One thing for sure, the man didn't play when it came to kissing her.

When she tucked her fingers into his waistband and attempted to pull him inside, he broke his mouth away. Disappointment flooded her immediately. "In addition to a kiss goodnight, I do recall you saying something about tucking me in." She bounced her brows twice.

"You have no idea how desperately I want to do just that, but I have surgery in the morning. I need to be focused. If I come inside, I'd be here all night." He pecked her gently, then shook his head. "You are a whole lot of sweet temptation." A pained expression slid across his face. "I have to go," he said, releasing her and backing away.

"That kiss. It felt like you were saying more than just goodnight," she said.

"I was. I was saying thank you."

Her brows bunched. "For what?"

Sadona couldn't stop laughing as Keith told her the story of how he'd briefly thought she and his good friend Craven Monroe had slept together, and the relief she'd witness on Keith's face. Yes, she knew Craven. They'd gone to high school together. He'd chased her for most of their junior year. But beyond that, they were practically strangers now. She could only recall having seen the man once or twice in passing since she'd returned home.

Keith gave her one tantalizing kiss. "Good night, sugar lips."

"Slept tight, Dr. Fremont."

"Dream about me, Ms. Lassiter."

No doubt she would.

10

Sadona couldn't imagine a more beautiful way to end an afternoon than relaxing in a hammock with Keith in his sprawling backyard, watching the sunset of all things. A warm breeze blew, causing ripples in the pond in the distance. The last few rays of sunlight danced against the surface of the water sparkling tiny bursts of light that forced her to squint a time or two.

She'd loved it here from the first time she'd visited. The rustic ranch-style home held lots of charm, but it was the lush fourteen acres that wooed her. Keith had told her he'd purchased the property for a steal from his uncle who'd retired to Florida.

"Do you hear that?" she asked.

"Hear what, babe?"

"Exactly. It's so peaceful. Nothing but birds chirping, leaves rustling, water sloshing. I love it here."

"I love it here, too. But you know what I love even more?"

Sadona's stomach fluttered, afraid of what was about to escape past Keith's lips. Surely, he wasn't going to say he loved *her*. They'd only been together a few months. But what if he did? What would she say? Yes, she had feelings for him—strong feelings—but it couldn't be love. Right?

Right, she told herself. Love didn't happen this fast.

"What?" she asked.

"Being here with you."

In her head, she blew a sigh of relief. However, there was a slight twinge of disappointment she couldn't quite explain. Or rather, refused to disclose. Had she wanted him to say he loved her?

No. That would have been ridiculous.

"And I love being here with you, too," she said, coming to her senses.

Keith kissed the crook of her neck and she tingled.

"Did you enjoy yourself today?" he asked.

Sadona shifted to eye the red and white checkerboard blanket and wicker basket sitting several feet away. Keith had surprised her with a picnic by the pond. It had been the best afternoon ever.

"I enjoyed it immensely," she said, tilting her head for a kiss.

As usual, he didn't disappoint. He rested a large hand on the side of her neck, pulled her mouth closer and kissed her thoroughly and completely. Breaking his mouth away, he stared down at her. She often wondered what went through his mind when he silently ogled her. Was it the same thing that traveled through her—how doggone happy he made her?

"I could kiss you forever and still not get

enough of your sugar lips."

Sadona kinda liked the idea of him kissing her forever. Kinda liked it a lot. She eased her head back to his chest, inched her hand under his shirt and ran her fingers over his six-pack.

"You make me happy, Sadona Lassiter. Real happy. A kind of happiness I haven't felt in a long time. Too long, if you asked Adda."

Sadona had learned that you really didn't have to *ask* Adda anything. Her opinions came freely. But she liked the blunt woman, because she seemed to take such good care of Keith.

"I don't want to lose you," he said.

Lose her? The choice of words, the hint of something in his tone made Sadona lift her head again. She studied him a moment, trying to get a read on the stern expression he wore. *Nothing*. "You're not going to lose me, Keith. Why do you think you would?"

His eyes held a troubled look that knotted her insides. It was familiar, similar to one Alec had given her right before he'd confessed to an affair. Her stomach churned at the idea of Keith being unfaithful.

"What is it, Keith? What are you trying to tell me?"

***

"Everything," Keith said, dragging a finger down the side of Sadona's worried face.

Her furrowed brow revealed her confusion. Understandable. He wasn't exactly making the most sense. But he was nervous as hell. He'd never felt this way about any woman, including the mother of his child.

"I don't understand, Keith."

He sat up the best he could in the wobbly contraption. "When we first met, I tried to fight my attraction to you, but it was much too strong."

Sadona followed suit. "Why?"

"Honestly, I wasn't sure I was ready for this. Ready for you, for us."

"What changed your mind?"

"You. I'm not sure if anyone has ever told you this before, but you're kinda irresistible."

Sadona smirked. "Flattery will get you everywhere."

Keith wrapped his arms around her and eased back down in the hammock.

Sadona pulled at the fabric of his shirt. "I tried to fight my attraction to you, too."

He gasped. "Whaaaaa? Say it ain't so."

Sadona pinched his nipple.

"*Oww*. You're so violent," he said in a nasally voice, then kissed the top of her head. "Well, I've got you now, Ms. Lassiter, and I'm not letting go."

"Well, Dr. Fremont, I wouldn't want it any other way."

An hour or so later, Keith had another surprise for Sadona. He led her inside, filled the bathroom with candles and ran her a hot bubble bath, then told her to relax while he handled something in the kitchen.

Granted, Keith wasn't much of a cook, but he didn't need to be. At least, according to the infomercial that had enticed him to order the electric pressure cooker. To be frank, he hadn't wholly believed the gadget was as versatile and simple to use as the dude on television had made it out to be—claiming home-cooked meals in minutes. But the man had been right. And Keith had a gorgeous, tender pot roast adorned with potatoes, onions, carrots and celery to prove it.

So that they wouldn't be disturbed, Keith placed Buddy and Baxter in the doggie playroom in the back of the house. Adding a few last minute touches to the dining room, he led Sadona in. Her jaw dropped scanning the ultra-romantic space. Judging by the look on her face, he'd done well.

A bouquet of fresh flowers sat in the center of the table. Calla lilies, gerbera daisies and hydrangeas—all of Sadona's favorites—framed by two tall taper candles. A bottle of Pinot Noir sat chilling in a silver bucket off to the side.

"Oh my God, Keith." She cupped her hands under her chin as if she were praying. "You did all of this...for me?"

"Whom else, sugar lips?" He loved the reserved smile she flashed every time he called her that. "You deserve to be treated like a queen. My queen."

Sadona cradled his face and came up on her

toes to kiss him. "It's so beautiful. And amazing. You're amazing. It smells fantastic." She rested her hands on her hips and slid him a narrow-eyed gaze. "I thought you said you couldn't cook."

"I'm full of surprises, baby."

"Yes, you are." She pressed her warm body against his. "Thank you. That you would take this time to do this means everything to me."

"You're welcome." He wrapped her in his arms, then dipped his head to kiss her. It wasn't the usual spine-twisting lip-lock he usually plastered on her, but it would have to do for now. He needed to remain focused. Ravishing her mouth like he wanted to would have certainly thrown him off his game.

"Is that all I get," Sadona said, her tempting lips curling into a pout.

"For now."

Pulling out a chair, he waited for her to ease down. Once she had, he slid it in place. After serving her, he took his seat. Intertwining their fingers, they bowed their heads for grace.

"Dear God, thank you for the food we're about to receive for the nourishment of our bodies. Thank you for this beautiful woman to share it with. For that, I'm most grateful. Amen."

When his head rose, the look on Sadona's face caused heat to blossom in his chest. An extreme amount of tenderness danced in her eyes, and it looked as if she could start bawling at any moment. He could handle many things, but a woman crying was not one of them.

Thankfully, no tears fell. *Whew*.

The roast was even more impressive than Keith had expected. It didn't rival any of the five-diamond meals Sadona had painstakingly prepared, but he was proud of what he'd produced. Sadona appeared satisfied, so the meal was a win in his book.

After dinner—two hours spent chatting about anything and everything under and above the sun—they tidied the kitchen, then moved into the living room. Keith dropped onto the sofa as if preparation and clean up had zapped all of his strength. But when Sadona straddled his lap, he experienced a wicked burst of energy.

When she guided his head back and dragged her tongue along his Adam's apple, a deep guttural sound rumbled in his chest. She kissed the crook of his neck, up the side, along his jawline and to his mouth.

"Now do I get that kiss?" she asked against his lips in a low, seductive tone.

"You get anything you want."

In one swift motion, he had her back-down on the area rug. Sadona's legs wrapped around his waist as if to make sure he didn't escape. She didn't have to worry about that. He wasn't going anywhere.

He stretched her arms over her head, then glided the tip of his fingers along the undersides of her arms. Fine bumps prickled her skin, and her blooming nipples pressed against the fabric of her blouse.

"I planned to have you for dessert. I hope that's okay," he said, cupping her breasts and rolling her taut nipples between his fingers.

Sadona's breath hitched, then seeped past her lips slowly. "More than okay."

As always, the mere hint at making love to Sadona made him hard as hell. His dick swelled and throbbed inside his briefs. Pinning her arms in place, he leaned into her and pressed his hardness against her core, rotating his hips slowly.

Sadona bit into her bottom lip. The move, plus the heated gleam in her eyes, suggested she wanted him just as much as he wanted her. It fluffed his ego.

"I hope this isn't your favorite shirt," he said.
"Why?"

A second later, he yanked it open, causing buttons to pop across the room like kernels of heated corn. Sadona yelped, then grinned. Dragging a finger down her torso, he unfastened her pants and slid the zipper down. Repositioning himself, he kissed along the band of the pink panties she wore. She squirmed and raised her hips slightly.

"Don't worry. I'm going to taste the hell out of you. But not just yet," he said.

A mix between a whimper and a sob escaped from her. The sound stirred his need. He kissed his way back up her body, stopping at her breasts and

JOY AVERY

freeing them from their lacy enclosure. A boom of appreciation rumbled in her chest.

"Have I told you how damn beautiful your breasts are?"

"Once or twice."

Wasting no more time, he captured one of her tight buds between his lips and sucked gently. Sadona cried out. One thing he loved just as much as her mouth were her large nipples, and so did his tongue. He circled, flicked, suckled. And when he felt he'd given that one enough attention, he moved to the opposite.

Finally relinquishing her breasts, he kissed her, making up for the lackluster one he'd given her earlier.

After several moments, Sadona tore her mouth away. "I want you, Keith. Now. Right now."

"Patience, sugar lips."

"I don't have any when it comes to making love to you."

He smirked, then removed her pants, keeping her panties in place. Through the damp fabric, he teased her with the tip of his tongue—just enough to build her anticipation, but not enough to send her over the edge.

Guiding her onto her stomach, he pressed his lips to the small of her back.

"*Mmm*," Sadona hummed.

Inching her panties down, he dragged his middle finger along the split of her ass, then sank the long finger inside her, making her groan deeply.

"Damn, baby. Did I get you this wet?"

"Y-yes."

He slowly moved the finger in and out of her. "I should do something about it, huh?"

"Damn right you should."

Maneuvering her onto her back, he buried his face between her legs and claimed her glistening womanhood as if he needed her juices to sustain life. Something broke inside him, releasing a greedy beast. He ate her madly, to the point of dizziness. But the spinning didn't stagger his performance.

He used his tongue in ways he'd never used it before. Feasted on her with an urgency he'd never known before. When she screamed his name and clawed at the rug, it heightened his determination. Several seconds later, she shattered, her body bucking wildly.

Pulling away, he practically ripped his clothes off, fell between her legs and drove into her with a primal force. "Jesus," he forced through clenched teeth.

Their bare connection nearly drove him insane. She was warm, silky and pulsing around him. A sliver of common sense crept in, demanding his immediate withdrawal.

"I need...to stop, baby. I'm not wearing anything." A mistake he never should have made. He always practiced safe-sex. But Sadona had a way of scrambling his brain. Especially when she was naked.

"Don't stop," Sadona said.

Did she really know what she was saying, or was the clutch of passion forcing her to render a decision she wouldn't have typically made? He desperately wanted to be the voice of reason, of better judgment, of self-control. Unfortunately, his commonsense faltered, then faded.

He withdrew, but only long enough to guide her onto her stomach and lift her hips to meet him. Sliding back into her wetness, he slammed into her until his own body trembled and refused to allow him to deliver another stroke.

She came.

Hard.

He came.

Even harder.

Sadona's muscles pulsed around him, milking him bone-dry. Unable to stay upright, he toppled over—his spent body half on Sadona, half on the rug. His chest rose and fell in quick succession and sweat beads rolled down his face and back.

"That was intense," Sadona said, her breathing as ragged as his.

"Hell yeah, it was. You tried to kill me, woman."

She washed a hand down his face, removing the wetness. "Would it have been worth it?"

"Absolutely."

They lay in silence for a long moment, just staring into each other's laden eyes. When Sadona traced his lips with her finger, he sucked the tip into his mouth. She giggled like a schoolgirl.

Sobering, her expression turned somber.

"You said you haven't smiled in a long time. Why?" she asked.

"I haven't had a reason to. Not until now."

Her expression lit into a warm smile. "Tell me about him, Keith. KJ."

The request took him by surprise, and a ping of sadness rushed through him. In the time they'd been together, he hadn't told her much about KJ and she hadn't asked. What prompted her curiosity now?

Keith fixed his mouth to say, "Later," but reconsidered. "He was smart, inquisitive and had a heart of gold."

"Like his father," Sadona said gently.

Like his father. Keith wanted to dispute her claim, but decided to simply accept the compliment.

"If I were having a bad day, the kid knew just what to do or say to make it better." He chuckled. "He loved waffles. He was addicted to them. Wanted them for breakfast, lunch and dinner. I haven't eaten one since he died."

Sadona glided a hand over his cheek. "Keep going."

Strangely, he could. "He loved baseball. Every so often I'd surprise him with tickets to watch the Durham Bulls play. You would have thought it was Christmas by the way his eyes would light up every single time we—" His voice cracked and he stopped briefly.

Sadona kissed the tip of his nose. The simple show of affection gave him the strength to continue. "Every single time we went. I asked him once why he enjoyed the games so much."

"What did he say?"

Keith swallowed the painful lump of emotion lodged in his throat. "He said it wasn't the games he loved so much; it was being there with me. KJ used to call me his hero. Truthfully, he was mine. That kid made me a better man. He was my world. Then...he was gone."

Overwhelmed, he rolled onto his back. As hard as he fought it, he couldn't keep his tears from falling. They streamed from the corner of his eyes. Sadona didn't attempt to pacify him with well-intended words, which he appreciated.

What she did was far more meaningful. She kissed his tears away. In that moment, he knew with absolute certainty he loved her.

11

Sadona took one look at her cell phone and sent the private caller to voicemail. One guess as to who it had been. Alec. She had no idea why—out of the blue—he'd started calling her again. When she hadn't taken any of his calls previously, he'd started blocking his number. As usual, he didn't leave a voicemail. More importantly, she didn't care.

She was too damn happy in her life to focus any of her energy on Alec. Sliding a glance to Keith, standing across the yard manning the grill with Nico, she smiled. Yep, too damn happy to focus any energy on Alec and his drama.

Lounging poolside in Nico and Gadiya's backyard was her second favorite comfort spot. The lake was her first. She was starting to develop a thing for water. Again, her eyes drifted across the yard to Keith, now having a laughing fit with Nico about something. Keith had molded right into their tight-knit circle. *Just like family*, Rana had said. Recalling her sister's words made her smile.

The white muscle T-shirt he wore showcased his well-toned arms, while the red board shorts exposed his powerful legs. Legs that delivered such delicious force. *Mmm, mmm, mmm.*

Smoke wafted from the grill and filled the air of the unmistakable aroma of good food. When her stomach growled, she prayed the food would be ready soon. The several pieces of fruit and cheese she'd eaten earlier weren't holding her. She'd had a big breakfast. Why was she so hungry?

Then it hit her. She'd worked the meal off. In her head, she replayed the moment Keith had pinned her against the wall and brought her to two powerful orgasms. Fire pooled in her belly at the memory. Now she was starving, but not for food.

Gadiya's voice filtered into her thoughts. Unfortunately, she hadn't heard a word she'd said.

"Are you listening to me?" Gadiya asked.

"Of course. What did you say?"

Gadiya shook her head. "Like I thought. I said, I noticed you were walking a little bow-legged when you arrived. Did you and Keith go horseback riding this morning?"

The mischievous look on Gadiya's face made Sadona burst into laughter. When Keith and Nico looked in their direction, Sadona covered her mouth to conceal her amusement.

"Hey, babe," Gadiya said, waving at her adoring husband. "I love you. And yes, we're chatting about the two of you. Mainly Keith."

Sadona's eyes grew wide, and she swatted at Gadiya.

"As long as it's good stuff, I'm okay with it," Keith said.

"Oh, it is. She's telling me about you taking her horseback riding this morning. Or was it bareback riding," Gadiya mumble out the side of her mouth to Sadona.

"Man, I didn't know you rode." Nico said, looking thrilled.

Keith, on the other hand looked utterly confused.

"I like horseback riding, but I prefer riding a camel," came from behind them.

He'd been so quiet, Sadona had almost forgotten Greenville was there. Greenville was a regular at the Dupree house. Since saving Nico's life by leading him safely from a burning building a while back, he'd become part of the family.

Sadona didn't know much about the man, other than he'd shown up in Mount Pleasance one day and had been there ever since and that he'd been homeless until Nico stepped in, making sure the man had a place to call home.

Wearing an army fatigue jacket, long-sleeved Henley shirt, dark denim jeans and cowboy boots, Sadona was surprised the man hadn't passed out.

Refocusing on Keith and Nico, Sadona waved a hand through the air. "Don't pay her any attention. Pregnancy hormones. She's delusional."

"And hungry," Gadiya added. "I'm always so freaking hungry. One more month and I can't wait." She tossed her hands in the air. "Thank you, Jesus."

They all laughed.

"Can I get a hotdog or something, babe? Your child is starving," Gadiya said, rubbing her humongous stomach.

Sadona wouldn't be convinced Gadiya wasn't having twins until she gave birth. Two babies could easily fit in there.

Nico loaded a plate with several items and Keith delivered it. Before walking away, he bent for a kiss. After a long peck, his eyes scanned the length of her body.

"Umph," he hummed, biting his bottom lip. "You make that bikini look amazing." He winked and strolled off.

Sadona had to admit, she did look pretty damn hot. Initially, she'd had reservations about wearing the emerald green two-piece—allowing her trouble area to be on display—but the second she recalled the way Keith always admired her naked body, all doubt faded. The man made her feel flawless at all times—even when she looked thrown away.

"He's right. You do look uh...maze...zing. And I hate you so much right now." Gadiya scrutinized herself. "I look like a yellow painted submarine," she said, stuffing a hot dog into her mouth.

"You look stunning. You're carrying a life inside of you. I'm not sure I've ever seen you more beautiful."

Gadiya's bottom lip trembled and tears clouded her eyes. "Really?"

Sadona squeezed her hand. "Yes, really."

Gadiya fanned her eyes. "These damn— *darn*—hormones. I cry every five seconds. Last night, I cried for an hour over endangered Steller sea lions. You better not be using seal oil in any of your products."

Sadona flashed her palms. "I'm not."

"Baby, you okay?"Nico asked.

"Hormones."

Sadona almost expected Gadiya's head to start spinning.

Gadiya jabbed a finger at Nico. "You did this to me."

"And I'm going to do it to you several more times."

Obviously, Nico was comfortable with toying with death.

"In your dreams, buster. One and done," Gadiya said, rolling her eyes away. "I'd give him a thousand babies if he wanted them," Gadiya whispered to Sadona.

"You two are too stinking perfect for each other."

"You and Keith are pretty stinking perfect for each other too."

Staring across at her man, Sadona's lips curled into a broad smile. Heat bloomed in her soul. The reason frightened her. *Love*. Dear God. Had she really allowed herself to fall in love with Keith? *When*? She tried her best to pinpoint the exact moment. She couldn't, because it felt as if she'd always loved him.

"And someone's in love," Gadiya said.

Her sister's claim broke her concentration. "Love? I'm not in love," she said in a hushed and urgent tone. Nothing had been confirmed. She'd only toyed with it in her head. Best to adamantly deny it for now.

"The lies you tell," Gadiya said. "But I wasn't referring to you."

Gadiya's gaze slid toward Keith and Sadona's followed. When their eyes connected, he tossed a sexy smile at her—a display of brilliant white against a canvas of molten hot chocolate. Butterflies performed a full-on choreographed performance in her stomach. She pressed a hand into her abdomen to cease the flash mob.

"I am," Sadona muttered, more for her own clarification than Gadiya's. "I am in love with him."

"I know already," Gadiya said. "Does he?"

After a fantastic evening spent with her family, Keith drove her home. Sadona hated that he wouldn't be staying, but didn't give him a hard time. His intentions were noble. He'd be relieving Adda from watch-duty at the clinic. He'd performed emergency surgery earlier. The next twenty-four hours were touch and go for the dog and Keith hadn't wanted to leave him unattended overnight.

Unfortunately, this meant he'd be spending the night on a sofa in his office, and she'd be spending it alone. That sucked. But she loved the way he cared for his patients.

Keith pulled into her driveway, put the vehicle in park, killed the engine and eyed her. Not with a look of admiration as he usually did, but with one of uncertainty and concern.

"What's wrong?" he asked.

Sadona's brows bunched. "Wrong?"

"You've been uncharacteristically quiet since we left Nico and Gadiya's place. Have I done or said something wrong?" He tossed up his hands defensively. "For the record, sugar lips slipped out."

Sadona laughed recalling how hard everyone had laughed when Keith had called her by the pet name at the dinner table. Sobering, she opened her mouth to speak, closed it, opened it again, closed it again. Finally finding her words, she said, "I...we have..." She turned away and blew a heavy sigh.

The words she thought she'd found disappeared beyond the fog of emotion clouding her brain. What if—

Keith brushed his thumb across her cheek. "Full-strength, never watered down, remember?"

Yeah, she remembered.

"I can handle anything you have to say to me, Sadona. I won't—"

"I love you," she blurted. Eyeing him, she said, "I'm...in love with you."

The smile slid from Keith's face. He stared silently at her for another few seconds, then got out of the vehicle without a word. Sadona's heart sank. Obviously, he *couldn't* handle anything she had to say to him.

Unfastening her seatbelt, she reached for the door handle. But before she could grip it, the door swung open. Keith snatched her from the seat. The move was so swift, so unexpected she gasped. When her back slammed against the vehicle, she yelped. In a flash, Keith's mouth smashed against hers. Once the initial shock had worn off, she relaxed and melted into the kiss.

Tightly, he gripped the sides of the off-shoulder denim dress she wore and ravished her mouth so deliciously, she burned with desire. All she wanted to do was quench this raging thirst brewing for him. If she hadn't been worried about her nosey neighbors, she would have unfastened his pants, pushed them below his hips and climbed onto the erection pressing into her stomach.

Obviously, Keith had similar elicit thoughts, because he opened the back passenger's side door, pulled her away from the hard surface of the SUV and urged her into the backseat.

She liked where this was headed.

It had been a long time since she'd made out in the backseat, her junior year of high school to be exact. She prayed this moment would go much farther than the one with Rebound Ricky had. That evening had come to an abrupt stop when her on-again, off-again star football player boyfriend had yanked Pretty Ricky from the black Toyota Camry and threatened to rip off both his arms and beat him with them if he ever so much as looked at her again.

Ricky hadn't.

On a comforting note, there was no one to

snatch Keith from the vehicle and threaten bodily harm. He was it. Her one and only. The thought made her all mushy inside.

Closing the door to stave off prying eyes, Keith maneuvered onto his knees, removed her panties and passed them to her. "Hold those for me," he said with a roguish grin.

Before she could reply, he planted his face between her legs and worked magic with his skillful tongue, bringing her to a powerful orgasm in no time at all. She battled to contain herself, but it felt too good. Sadona cried out, hoping her neighbors hadn't heard her and called the police. That would have been embarrassing.

Sliding into the seat adjacent her, Keith freed himself. The sight of his manhood—long, thick and ready—thrilled her to no end. Climbing into his lap, she effortlessly slid down his shaft. Keith pinched his eyes closed, reclined his head against the rest and swore several times under his breath.

With measured, methodical movements, Sadona worked him into a frenzy. Dipping forward, she dragged her tongue along the column of this neck. He tasted like salt, oak chips, and grill smoke. She swore the move caused him to swell even larger inside her. Eager to ride him like one would a mechanical bull, she took her time instead.

Up.

Down.

Hips 'round and 'round.

Keith drew in a sharp breath, then rested his

strong hands on her ass, stopping her motion. The move was akin to snatching a milk bottle from a starving baby's mouth. While she didn't burst into tears, she did pout.

"What's wrong?" she asked. The faint light from the street lamp allowed her to see that look in his eyes. The one he got right before he intended to say something serious.

"I love you, too," he said.

"You don't have to say it because I—"

"I love you Sadona Lassiter. And I say that of my own free will."

The spark in his eyes was so intense, so sincere her heart double-tapped in her chest. "Okay."

She lowered her mouth to his and they kissed gently, slowly. Keith's grip on her ass tightened, and he began guiding her movements.

Up.

Down.

Hips 'round and 'round.

Sadona jerked away from his mouth and pressed the palms of her hands into the roof of the vehicle, feeling the onset of an orgasm. Allowing her head to fall back, she moaned in pleasure. When Keith's warm, wet mouth closed over her aching nipple, she teetered dangerously closer to the edge.

A short time later, they came together in a barrage of cries, moans, groans, and swears. Sadona fell against Keith's chest, burying her face in the crook of his damp neck, her breathing ragged and so was his. Those strong arms wrapped securely around her, making her feel...protected.

When Keith's cell phone rang, he grumbled. "Adda. Wondering where I am. She has a hot date tonight."

"You'd better go. I don't want her blaming me for keeping you detained."

"Oh, it's all your fault. And that's exactly what I'm going to tell her.

Sadona nipped his neck gently. "You better not."

"Ow."

Gliding her tongue across the area where she'd afflicted the alleged *pain* made Keith moan.

"Stop that, woman," he said in a throaty voice. "You're going to wake him up again."

Sadona pressed a kiss to his neck, then reared back to eye him. "Call me when you get to the clinic, so I'll know you made it there safely."

"Look at you, all worried about me and stuff." He pressed a kiss to one corner of her mouth, then the other, then pecked her on the lips. "I will. I'll walk you to the door."

"And waste another two minutes? Heck, no. You better get to Adda. I can make it to my porch alone. I promise not to talk to strangers."

Keith laughed, then brushed an unruly hair behind her ear. "Let me hear you say it one more time."

Sadona ran a hand over his head, then kissed

his forehead. "I love you, Keith Fremont. And you're going to hear it plenty more times."

12

Waving to Keith—who'd refused to pull away until she'd stepped inside—Sadona blew him a kiss, then closed and locked the door. Buddy greeted her, wagging his tail and panting like seeing her brought him the greatest joy in the world. But she understood. She couldn't imagine her life without this little fellow. "Hey, boy. I've missed you, too."

After Keith had called to let her know he'd safely made it to the clinic, she showered, grabbed a bite to eat and spent some time on the floor with her best friend—wrestling playfully, tossing the red ball he couldn't get enough of, eagerly accepting his generous doggie kisses.

"Okay. Let's watch a little TV before bed, shall we?"

Buddy barked his agreement.

Sadona stretched out on the couch, flicked to one of the animal stations and patted a free spot for Buddy to join her. The man surfing with his dog held his attention. Maybe because the dog on the screen could have been his twin.

"Don't even think about it. I'm not taking you surfing."

Buddy whined and rested his head on her hip.

Sadona's eyes drifted closed several times, but she was determined to stay awake.

Two hours later, the sound of the Buddy alarm

startled her out of a nightmare. She was being chased by a rabid dog two times bigger than Cujo. Her heart raced as she struggled to catch her breath.

Tossing a glance at the wall clock, her brow furrowed. Who would be visiting her at ten at night? Panic set in when she thought about Gadiya and how she'd been having Braxton Hicks contractions. She calmed when she realized Nico would have called if there were a problem, not wasted time coming by.

That left only one person. *Keith*. A smile curled her lips as she hurried to the door, yanking it open. The joy she'd felt just a minute ago faded instantly when her eyes locked with her visitor. It hadn't been a nightmare she'd had, it had been a premonition.

"Alec?"

What the hell was he doing here? Freshly groomed, he wore a tailored black suit like he'd just left an important function. The top two buttons of his crisp white shirt were unfastened. He looked...good. Maybe even a level above good. But he'd always been able to garner attention from the opposite sex. That had been part of the problem.

When Buddy snarled at Alec, Sadona sent him to his bed. Thank goodness for Keith's training abilities. They had made Buddy quite obedient. After he settled onto his bed, she refocused on Alec. "What are you doing here?"

"I..." He swayed, then rested against the doorframe as though standing had become a burden.

Sadona leaned in close, getting a whiff of alcohol. Bourbon, if she had to guess. "Have you been drinking?"

"Just a little," Alec said, massaging his temple.

Her gaze slid to the wild manner he'd pulled into her driveway. A few more inches and the front end of his vehicle would have been in her trunk.

"One, maybe two drinks," he continued.

"And you're driving? How stupid can you be, Alec? You work in the district attorney's office for Christ sakes."

He ran a hand over his close-cut jet-black hair. "I needed to talk to you. You weren't answering my calls."

When he reached out to touch her, she swatted him away. "What are you doing *here*, Alec?"

"I was supposed to get married today. I screwed up. Again."

Ah. That explained the sharp look. Sadona waited for the news to trigger something inside her. It didn't. Not a single part of her was affected by the news. Uninterested in how he'd screwed up, she said, "Again, Alec, what are you doing here?"

He shrugged. "At the last minute, I couldn't go through with it. I couldn't pledge my love to another woman when I'm still in love with you. "

Had it been six months ago, she would have

slammed the door in his face if he'd shown up spouting such foolishness. But she'd grown. Taking his arms, she said, "Come in and sit down before you fall over. You're drunk and have no idea what you're saying."

Alec snatched his arm away. "I know exactly what I'm saying. I'm saying I want you back, baby. Please take me back. I'm sorry for hurting you."

He dropped to his knees and threw his arms around her so forcefully, she stumbled back. Obviously, Buddy thought she was in trouble, because he raced across the room, locked down on Alec's jacket and attempted to haul him away. It was the most endearing thing ever.

"Buddy, no!"

Buddy's mission to get Alec off of her was accomplished. Alec fell over onto the floor, squirming in an attempt to escape Buddy's wrath. Buddy was Team Keith. And so was she. Apparently determined to assert dominance, Buddy took a souvenir—Alec's entire jacket pocket—before retreating back to his bed.

"You need to put that vicious rat in a cage."

The only rat there was Alec, but name-calling wouldn't accomplish anything. "He's at home. You're not." She stood over Alec, her arms crossed over her chest. "I'm not taking you back, Alec. But of course, you knew that. And I won't give you a pep talk to make you feel better about yourself, because I'm no longer your cheerleader. I've moved on and I'm happy."

A look of surprise spread across his face. Had he thought she would spend the rest of her day sitting around sulking over him?

"There's someone else?" he said.

She hesitated a moment, but finally said, "There's *someone.* No *else.*"

"I see." He eyed her a moment. "That's great. That's...so great. I'm glad you've found happiness."

She hadn't believed that for one second. She knew this man. The idea that he wouldn't get what he wanted had to be drilling a hole in him. However, he was doing such an excellent job at concealing his displeasure, for a second, she considered that maybe the competitive Alec she'd known had—dare she say it—changed.

He struggled to get off the floor. "I don't want to cause any trouble. I'll go."

Didn't want to cause trouble? This was the same man who'd kept making up excuses why he couldn't sign the divorce papers. What kind of game was he playing?

Sadona sighed heavily, then took his arms to help guide him up. "I'm not going to allow you to endanger someone's life by driving drunk, Alec. You're going to sleep this off. First thing in the morning, you're going to get back in your car and go home. And we're both going to forget this night ever happened."

Sadona knew she was doing the right thing. So why did it feel as though she'd just unlocked the gates of hell?

"That's probably for the best. Like I said, I don't want to cause you any trouble."

She kicked herself for not yet having ordered a bed for the guest room. She contemplated making Alec a pallet on the floor next to Buddy, but abandoned the thought. Yep, she'd definitely become a much better person.

"You can sleep in my bed," she said. If she left him in the same room as Buddy, she was sure Buddy would rip him apart. She didn't need the increase in her homeowner's premium.

"Okay," he said. "I promise you won't know I'm there."

Sadona nearly barked a laugh. "I'm not sharing a bed with you, Alec. I'll take the sofa. Follow me."

Layering one side of the mattress with towels—because Alec sweated like a horse when he drank—she gave herself a pat on the back. If anyone had told her she'd one day be able to show him this much compassion, she would have laughed in their face. Alec captured her hand when she started out the room. She should have known he wouldn't make this simple for her. He never did.

"Thank you, Sadona," he said, "for showing me kindness I probably don't deserve."

Probably?

He released her. She managed a lazy smile, then continued out the room. Maybe Alec really had changed. The Alec she'd known rarely showed gratitude. While it was appreciative, it did little to move her.

While it was probably more comfortable—and smarter—to just keep Alec's visit to herself, she didn't want to start their relationship off shrouded in secrets. So, the first thing Sadona did when she returned to the living room was give Keith a call to let him know about her temporary houseguest.

***

When Keith cracked his eyes open a little after seven a.m., it took him a second or two to recall he was on the sofa in his office. On his back, he draped his arm across his forehead and closed his eyes again. Sleeping on this lumpy and unforgiving sofa had not been how he'd wanted to spend his Saturday night. Waking up to Sadona's soft body had been the far better option.

Swinging his legs over the sofa, he winched at the stiffness lingering in his muscles. He rolled his shoulders several times to work out the soreness. What he needed was Sadona's delicate fingers kneading into his flesh. She gave the best massages.

Leaning forward, he removed his cell phone from the small table. Damn. He'd missed three calls from Sadona. Clearly, he'd slept harder than he'd thought. Accessing the voicemail, he entered his code. But before the message began, the alarm system chirped, and the front door alert chimed, signaling someone had entered.

Keith tossed the phone aside, rushed to his

feet and grabbed the aluminum bat he'd placed in the corner after the clinic had been burglarized a few years ago by junkies looking to get high. He crept from the office, bat raised. Opting for the element of surprise, he jumped from around the corner and yelled, "Freeze," hoping the power of suggestion convinced the intruder he had a gun instead of just a bat.

The assault was swift—a fist to the stomach and a knee to the groin—Keith never even got the chance to swing the slugger. It fell to the floor, and he dropped to his knees, cupping his throbbing balls.

"Oh, shit," he forced through clenched teeth. At that moment, he welcomed death.

"Lawd, Sweet Jesus."

The voice was familiar. Finding enough strength to lift his head, Adda's presence both relieved and surprised him. She'd apparently paid damn good attention in the self-defense class he'd gifted her a few months back. Maybe he should consider taking it himself.

"Adda Belle, are you trying to kill me?" he said in a high-pitched tone.

"Why the hell you jumping out from behind walls like the damn boogie man?"

"I thought you were a junkie looking for meds," he strained out.

"Maybe next time, try the strong, silent approach," she said, helping him to his feet.

Keith bent at the waist and rested his hands

on his thighs, waiting for the pain to subside. "I was going for the element of surprise."

"Well...*surprise*."

"Were you a boxer in a past life? You have one helluva punch."

"Out of eight children, I was the only girl." She clapped him on the back. "A little ice and you'll be fine. Man up. Have Sadona kiss it and make it better."

Keith managed a shaky laugh. "I'll be sure to tell her you said that."

"I ain't scared."

Standing upright, he rested a hand against the wall. "What are you doing here?"

"I came to relieve you. My date didn't end like I wanted it to last night. All that fool wanted to do was talk about that beat-up white pickup he drives. Since I didn't wake up with a man in my bed, I figured Sadona wouldn't mind waking up to you in hers."

The idea of sliding into bed with Sadona soothed the discomfort in his crotch. She was a hard sleeper so she probably wouldn't even feel him ease in behind her. *The element of surprise*. He just hoped it turned out better than it had with Adda. He laughed to himself. Why wouldn't it?

With Baxter enjoying a sleepover at Craven's place, he wouldn't have to rush home. He could spend hours making love to Sadona. Oh, yeah. This was going to be an amazing day.

"You don't have to stay, Adda. Aloysius is

doing fine. He's out of the woods."

"Excellent. Well, in that case, I'm going to Melba's Diner. Get me some real food." She placed her hands on her wide hips. "Can you believe that fool took me to a vegan restaurant? Do I look like a vegetarian to you?"

"A vegan and a vegetarian aren't the—" He stopped, noting the narrow-eyed gaze she was giving him. That was his cue. "Nope. You don't look like a vegetarian."

"Did you just call me fat?"

Keith eyed her dumbly, contemplating his next move carefully. "Have I told you how much I love you lately?"

Adda's stone-faced expression cracked and a smile shined through. She dismissed him with a hand. "Get out of here and go get you some."

There was truly no replacement for Adda Belle. Kissing her on the forehead, he said, "Sorry you didn't get any last night. Don't give up."

"Do you want me to kick you in the nuts again?"

"No, ma'am, I do not."

A short time later, Keith arrived at Sadona's. He used the spare key she kept inside a hideaway rock on the porch. Buddy rushed across the floor to greet him, then looked past him and whined as if not seeing his playmate trot in pained him.

"Sorry, boy. Baxter's not with me. I'll get him later and you guys can run around the lake. How does that sound?"

Buddy barked, then returned to his bed, grabbing a strip of black fabric along the way.

Keith confiscated it. "Oh, no. Last thing we want is you swallowing this." He scrutinized the damp, chewed-up material. "Whatever this is."

He noticed the blanket and pillow on the sofa, but didn't give it much thought, since Sadona was always falling asleep there. Moving gingerly into the near pitch-black bedroom, he undressed and slid in behind Sadona. Draping his arm around her caused instant alarm.

"What the fu—"

He scuffled his way out of the bed, misstepped and hit the floor. He sprung up as if he had a spring attached to his ass. The man in Sadona's bed darted out with equal urgency. Flicking on the light, Keith redressed with haste. However, dude didn't seem bothered by standing there in his underwear in front of a stranger.

"Who the hell are you?" Underwear Man asked.

"Who the hell are you?" Keith retorted.

Confidently, he said, "Sadona's husband."

The words froze Keith in place.

Sadona's husband?

Keith had heard him clearly but was still having trouble processing it. The man's words confused, hurt, and angered him. Finally thawing from his stupor, he said, "*Ex*-husband, don't you mean?"

Or had Sadona lied to him all this time about

being divorced? No, she wouldn't have done that. But hey, he wouldn't have expected her to have another man in her bed either. Yet, here they were.

"Am I?" he asked, his expression unreadable.

Keith ground his teeth hard enough to turn them into dust. "Where's Sadona?"

The man shrugged. "Maybe she stepped out to get breakfast. It was a rough night. Who did you say you were, again?"

"Nobody."

Keith escaped from the room. He yanked the front door with enough force to take it off the hinges. Sadona—still holding onto the knob—half stumbled, half fell inside, dropping the bag she'd been carrying.

"Keith."

His eyes lowered to the plastic mini mart bag on the floor. Obviously, she *had* gone to get them breakfast after their rough night. His heated gaze landed on her. Staring into her eyes, visions of her moaning and rolling in the covers with her ex-husband filled his head and clogged his rational thinking. He brushed past her and practically leaped down the stairs.

"Keith, wait."

He stopped abruptly and Sadona bounced off his back. Whipping around to face her, he said, "Wait? Wait?" He nodded wildly, then forcefully crossed his arms over his chest. "Okay, Sadona. I'm waiting. Waiting for you to explain to me why your ex-husband—a man you claimed to despise—is in your house."

"He—"

"Waiting for you to explain to me why your ex-husband is standing in your bedroom in his damn underwear."

"Last night—"

"Waiting for you to explain to me why the hell your ex-husband was in your bed."

This time she remained silent and just stared at him.

"I'm waiting for you to explain to me why you're driving his car." Because the black sedan wasn't there when he first arrived. "Waiting for you to explain to me why you're buying him breakfast. Waiting for you to explain to me why he doesn't know you have a man. Waiting for you to explain to me why—"

"Keith!" she yelled in an obvious attempt to wrangle him in. "I'm trying to explain all of it, but you won't let me."

"There shouldn't be shit to explain in the first place, Sadona." He turned and started away again.

Sadona moved in his path and blocked his escape. "You're going to listen to me, Keith Fremont. I left you a—"

"He said you two had a rough night. What did that mean?"

Her face scrunched. "What?" She shook her head. "I'm not sure what lies Alec told you, but I swear—"

"Sadona!" Keith shifted away to regain his

composure. Calming his tone, he continued, "I know what I just saw. You could swear on a stack of bibles, and I still wouldn't believe a single word you're about to say to me."

Sadona flashed a bewildered look that suggested she had absolutely no idea how to respond to what he'd just said to her. Pain danced in her eyes, letting him know he'd hurt her. Regret gnawed at him and, for a second, he considered that he might have been acting unfairly. But when Alec appeared at the doorway, something shattered inside him.

"We should take a break." The pain that shot through him from saying the words nearly crippled him, but they were necessary.

Sadona's voice was level when she said, "Just like that? Twenty-four hours ago you told me you loved me and now you're going to end things like this, Keith?"

Tears glistened in her eyes, but she blinked them away before they had a chance to fall. It was all he could do to not reach out and pull her into his arms. Another vision of her moaning underneath Alec helped him refocus. Stepping around her, he hurried to his SUV.

She didn't pursue him this time.

Sliding behind the steering wheel, he cranked the engine, but he couldn't pull away. Sitting there a second or two, he fought the urge to glance in her direction. Ultimately deciding another glimpse of her would only shatter his heart more, he popped the vehicle into gear and drove away.

13

Lounging on her sofa with her sisters, Sadona could feel both sets of their probing eyes on her. For the past two weeks, they'd stuck to her like wet leaves on glass. What did they think she would do if they didn't show up every day, crack up? If she'd gotten through a divorce in her right mind, she could definitely get over Keith.

Her bottom lip quivered slightly just thinking his name, but she refused to shed one single tear over him. He didn't deserve them. The way he'd treated her, so cold. You didn't treat the person you supposedly love so cruel. How could she have ever believed he cared for her? Why was she always picking the wrong men?

Honestly, she had thought Keith was different. Unfortunately, she'd been bamboozled by love again. It wouldn't get a third time to make a fool of her.

Rana touched her arm and she flinched. "Are you okay?"

"I'm fine," Sadona said, forcing a smile. She didn't need Keith Fremont. Didn't need his touch. Didn't need his kisses. She had Buddy, and his love was genuine. What more did she need? She eyed Buddy across the room, sprawled out in his usual carefree manner. God, was she really planning her future around a dog? *Pathetic.*

Gadiya popped several cubes of cheese into her mouth. "I know you're sad now, but—"

"Sad? Why would I be sad over the man who refused to even give me an opportunity to explain?"

"I just meant—"

"Why would I miss a jerk who would believe I'd cheat on him with my trifling ex?"

"That's—"

"Why would I have actually thought falling in love with him could ever be a good idea?"

"Maybe you—"

"Why would I have ever believed he truly loved me?"

"Because—"

"Why—" She paused, her words catching in her throat. "Why does it hurt so much?" A single tear slid down her face, and she slapped it away. Forget Keith Fremont. "He doesn't deserve my tears and he doesn't deserve me. I blame myself for believing that love could be so easy. I should have known Keith was too good to be true."

Rana hugged her on one side and Gadiya attempted to hug her on the other, but her belly got in the way. Having her sisters near was all the therapy she needed. They would make sure she got through another heartache. As much as she hated to admit it, she still loved Keith, but she also knew with time that would fade. She hoped it happened sooner than later, because missing him was crippling her.

"I have to go," Gadiya said.

"Go?" Sadona and Rana said in unison.

"I totally forgot there's something I needed to take care of. For Nico," she added, then attempted to rock to a stand.

The spectacle gave Sadona some much-needed amusement. She and Rana laughed, then came to their baby sister's aid.

"How in the heck do you fit behind the steering wheel?" Rana asked jokingly.

Uh-oh, Sadona thought, when Gadiya's bottom lip trembled.

"Are you trying to make me cry?" Gadiya said. "I know I'm the size of Texas. And all I can wear are these huge tent dresses." She slapped at the stylish emerald green button-front dress she wore, then burst into tears. "I'm sorry. I'm sorry," she said.

It was Gadiya's turn to stand in the sister's circle of love. They both wrapped one arm around her and each placed their free hand on her belly.

"How many times do we have to tell you how beautiful you are? I would kill for that radiant glow you have," Sadona said. She would have also killed to be carrying a child. But she'd come to terms with that never happening. Gadiya didn't know how truly blessed she was. A man who loved her. A child on the way. All the things Sadona longed for but appeared she would never have.

"Whoa! He's kicking," Sadona said, her mood instantly improving at the feel of life inside her sister. "He's moving a lot."

"He sure is," Rana said. "It must be all of this positive energy."

"Or he knows he only has two more weeks on the inside," Sadona said.

Gadiya sniffled several times. "It's the hot wings. He loves them." She snagged one from the platter and practically sucked the meat off the bone.

Making sure Gadiya got to her vehicle safely, Sadona and Rana returned inside, each taking a corner of the sofa and curling up. They were quiet for a long time until Rana broke the unbearable silence that had allowed thoughts of Keith to swarm Sadona's thoughts—despite how hard she'd fought it.

"You can stop pretending now," Rana said. "I know you're trying to hold it together in front of Gadiya, but it's just the two of us here now. I know you miss him."

Dammit, why couldn't Rana have allowed her to quietly waddle in her sorrows? "I hate Alec, Rana. I don't like using that word, but when I think about him, it's the only term that fits. I showed him kindness and in return he spits in my face."

"You're just angry, Sa. You don't mean that."

"Oh yes, I do. He swears he didn't tell Keith we'd slept together, but I know he did. What's worse, Keith believed his lies. He believed a stranger over the woman he shares the bed with most nights." Sorrow moved through Sadona. Hadn't she meant anything to him? How could he walk away without looking back?

Rana shook his head. "I wouldn't be so sure about that."

Sadona scoffed. "Oh, he believed it. If not, why hasn't he reached out to me? The woman he supposedly loves. Love endures all things, right?"

"Keith loves you, Sa. No doubt in my mind. The way he looks at you is the same way daddy used to look at mommy, like she was his entire universe." Rana's folded her arms across her chest. "Would you have talked to him if he had reached out?"

Sadona flashed a defiant expression. After the way he'd treated her, probably not.

"I love you, big sis, but you can be stubborn as hell at times," Rana said with a chuckle. "Especially when you're all in your feelings. Like now." She bumped Sadona playfully. "Keith's angry and hurt. And I know you don't want to hear this, but he has a right to be."

Sadona sat up with urgency. "You think I'm wrong for not allowing Alec to drive intoxicated, potentially killing someone?"

"No, but Keith doesn't know the reason why Alec was here, Sa. All he knows is that your ex-husband was practically naked and in your bed. And I'm sure he doesn't care why he was there. He. Was There. Period. Even if he wanted to believe nothing happened between the two of you, the evidence is damning."

Okay, she could give Rana that one. It had

looked suspicious. But still…

"Judging by Keith's reaction to the situation, he's been hurt in his past," Rana said. "Maybe this triggered something inside him."

Relaxing back, Sadona sighed. "It wasn't like I was hiding anything, Ra. I left him a message, which he obviously never listened to. I tried to explain and he walked away. He didn't believe in me—in us—enough to just listen. That's what hurts most. If he would have just listened, he, of all people, would have understood."

Sadona hadn't shared with either of her sisters about Keith losing his only child to a drunk driver. In her mind, she'd been honoring Keith, honoring his son's memory by not allowing that to potentially happen to another family. Unfortunately, he would never know this.

"Give him time, Sa-Sa."

"So, I'm just supposed to sit around waiting for him to come to his senses, realize I love him, and know I would never betray him like that?" Nope, not going to happen.

Rana flashed a tender expression. "Love endures all things, right?"

"Yes, but love isn't uncertain," Sadona shot back.

And in her mind, Keith had shown her just how unsure he was about them.

***

After several prior attempts Keith finally decided to listen to the message Sadona had left him a couple of weeks ago. Up until now, he'd refused to listen to it as if his stubbornness would in some way punish Sadona. He'd only been punishing himself, because he was sure the sound of her voice could have softened the blow of being without her.

Keith wasn't sure why, but his thumb hovered over the button that would play it. Could he handle hearing her voice—even if it was only a recording?

Damn, he missed that woman. It haunted him how much he still loved her. But it didn't surprise him the impact of losing her would have on him. He'd tried his damnedest not to think about her, but he was rarely successful. Everything reminded him of Sadona. His living room, the kitchen, the backyard, the lake—especially the lake. Her favorite spot.

"Shit. Quit doing this to yourself," he mumbled. *Just press the damn button*. Before he could, pounding sounded at his front door. "What the…?"

Grabbing the closest thing to him—a veterinarian of the year trophy he'd won last year—he cautiously neared the door. Peeping out, he chuckled, seeing Gadiya's belly before he saw her. She really did look as though she were having twins.

Her unannounced visit troubled him. Replacing the trophy, he opened the door.

"Gadiya?" Her puffy, bloodshot eyes and frown made his stomach do backflips. If anything had happened to Sadona... He didn't even want to think about that. Though they were no longer together, he still loved her in a way that frightened him.

"Sadona's divorce left her broken. I didn't ever think she'd trust in love again, which I thought was so sad because she deserves to be loved and someone deserves to receive the bounty of love she has to give." She flashed a delicate smile. "Then you came along and made her soooo happy."

Keith glanced down briefly when Baxter brushed against his legs. Maybe he'd heard Sadona's name and assumed she was there. He loved and missed her, too.

"Slowly, I watched my sister go from a piece of dull latex to a beautiful work of balloon art. Then *pop*! You deflated her."

Both Keith and Baxter jerked.

He assumed Gadiya's colorful analogy stemmed from the fact that she was a balloon artist. Not wanting to upset her, he spoke gently. "Gadiya, with all due—" Her bottom lip quivered as if she were about to bawl and he froze. *No, no, no*, he warned quietly. *Please don't do that*. As if she'd heard his inner plea, she straightened her shoulders and continued.

"This *is* my business. She's my sister and her happiness will *always* be my business. Someone deserves Sadona's love...but it's not you. You, sir, are an asshole. And I pity you. I pity you for not recognizing the good thing you had. Nope, you don't deserve my sister. Good day."

Turning in dramatic fashion, the green dress she wore swelled with air. She started away, but apparently had a change of heart. Facing him again, she jabbed her finger at him and narrowed her eyes.

"And another thing—" She stopped abruptly, her hands framing her stomach. "Ooo."

A stream of liquid ran down Gadiya's legs and puddled on the porch. Keith drew back like he'd blindly touched something cold and slimy. Baxter ran off so fast, he couldn't get traction on the hardwood floor and slipped and slid his way inside the house.

Gadiya's eyes widened. "Uh-oh. My water just broke." A second later, she screamed, "Yes!" and pumped her fist into the air.

"Let me grab my keys and I'll drive you to the hospital," Keith said. Gadiya's lips parted, but he cut her off before she could object. "Your family would kill me if I allowed you to drive yourself. So, yes, I am driving you there."

She rolled her eyes away and started down the stairs. "Fine."

On the drive to the hospital, Gadiya contacted Nico. Keith listened to her gently explain why she'd visited him—to set some things straight, she'd said. He laughed to himself when she yelled, "Because I'm pregnant and emotional." Then she started to cry. Lord, her tear ducts should be spotless.

After ending the call with Nico, she contacted Sadona and filled her in—omitting him entirely. *My water broke on Keith's front porch* became *my water broke while I was out handling some business*.

Maybe Gadiya thought if she mentioned his name Sadona wouldn't show at the hospital. *No way that would have happen*. Those Lassiter Sisters were spandex tight.

A short time later, they arrived at Mount Pleasance General. Nico was waiting for them out front. He rushed to the vehicle, yanked the door open and showered his wife with kisses. It was a beautiful sight to see two people care for each other the way these two did.

His soul mate, Nico had called Gadiya. Keith hadn't been convinced soul mates existed until he'd found Sadona. At one point, he'd been convinced she had been his.

"Thank you, man," Nico said.

"I didn't do anything, but you're welcome."

Gadiya turned toward him, her expression kind. "Thank you, Keith, and I'm sorry."

"No worries. It was the hormones talking."

Her expression darkened, and it kinda scared him.

"I'm apologizing for inconveniencing you and for leaving a mess on your porch, not for what I said. That was from the heart, not hormones." She slid out of the SUV.

Rana rushed through the electric doors, followed by Sadona, who stopped shy of approaching the vehicle when she locked eyes with him. Their connection was like a jolt of limitless energy. It shot all through his system, recharging him and sparking memory after memory. He turned away, unable to withstand its potency any longer.

"You coming inside, man?" Nico asked.

"I...can't stay," he said, despite wanting to. But he couldn't. Hospitals brought back unpleasant memories. "I'll have my buddy follow me to your place to drop off Gadiya's car. I'll put the key above the visor."

"Thanks again, man. I owe you."

"Just keep me posted. That'll be payment enough. And congrats."

"Will do. Thanks."

Unable to resist, he slid his eyes to Sadona one last time. Sadness danced on her usually jovial face and his heart ached. Nico's words from a few months back rang in his head. *That Lassiter woman magic is real and potent. Once Sadona works it on you, there's no breaking the spell.* Keith had no idea how right Nico had been until this very moment.

Maybe he should... Before he finished the thought, Sadona rolled her eyes away and disappeared back inside. *Damn.*

Pulling away from the curb, he couldn't get Sadona off his mind. Seeing her was like the freshest breath of air he'd ever taken. When they'd locked gazes, he hadn't been able to label what he'd seen in her eyes. It wasn't hate, but not quite admiration, either.

In his mind—and he was fairly certain it had been playing tricks on him—she'd appeared disappointed when he'd declined Nico's invitation to stay. Had she been?

Not staying now felt like the second biggest mistake he'd made, the first being losing her. But he was still so damn angry and hurt and confused. Despite how much he loved her, those three things paralyzed him to his next move.

Maybe Gadiya had been right. Maybe he didn't deserve Sadona. "You had to walk into my damn life," he said, striking the steering wheel.

He cursed himself for not resisting Sadona from the start. But, in his defense, it hadn't been possible. Something had drawn him to her. That same something continued to draw him to her.

Giving his overworked brain a rest, he phoned Craven, asked him to meet him at his place to follow him over to Nico's to drop off Gadiya's vehicle, then tried his best to keep his mind off of Sadona. Unfortunately, his thoughts were determined to drive him insane.

Tapping into voicemail, he finally played the message Sadona had left him a while back. The instant her delicate voice filled the cabin, he relaxed. That was what she always did for him, soothed him when he was frazzled.

"Hey, babe. It's me. I really don't want to

leave this on your voicemail but looks like I have no other choice."

There was a brief pause before Sadona started speaking again.

"My ex-husband showed up at my place tonight. Intoxicated. As bad as I want to toss him out on his ass, I can't allow him to get back on the road in this condition. I know you understand why."

Keith's thoughts shifted to KJ.

"He's going to sleep here tonight, but will be gone first thing in the morning. I'm going to take the sofa. Since Buddy has already tried to rip him to pieces once, they probably shouldn't be in the same room together."

Keith smirked at the visual that materialized in his head. He owed Buddy a treat.

"Anyway," Sadona continued. "Don't get alarmed."

Keith's brows bunched. *Don't get alarmed*?

Sadona laughed softly. "Okay, with the nature of the situation I know you're going to get a little alarmed. But trust in your sugar lips. Trust in us. I know what it feels like to be betrayed, and I would *never* do that to you."

Trust in us. The words were like a sucker punch to his gut, because he'd done the complete opposite. He'd placed all of his trust into a past that had left him empty, instead of in the woman who kept him full.

"This is not an ideal situation for either of us,

Keith, but know that I love you and would never do anything to jeopardize what we're building. Which is something extremely beautiful, by the way." She sighed. "Well, that's it. Heck, that's enough. I'll try calling you again a little later. I really would prefer talking to you directly. But in the meantime, I love you, Dr. Fremont."

The line went dead.

Keith veered onto the side of the road, his SUV kicking up a cloud of dust behind him. Putting the vehicle into Park, he fell back against the seat. Sadona had told him everything. All about her ex-husband being at her place, all about him being in her bed. Everything.

14

After spending all day and most of the night at the hospital, Sadona was finally on her way home. She was exhausted, but she could have spent eternity holding her niece. All seven pounds, six ounces of her. One of her greatest disappointments was that she would never know how it felt to feel a precious life growing inside of her.

Given the opportunity, there were so many things in her past she'd change. Like not allowing Alec to dictate whether or not she became a mother. Spending precious years loving a man who didn't know how to be loved. Denying her own happiness for so long.

"No use dwelling on the past. What's done is done."

Sadona's eyes narrowed on the SUV parked at the curb in front of her house. *Keith*? What was he doing here? Pulling into the driveway, she spotted him sitting on her front step. For whatever reason, she tossed a glance at herself in the rearview mirror before exiting.

Keith didn't acknowledge her when she approached. The behavior was odd, but she didn't dwell on it. She was more interested in learning why he was sitting in the dark on her porch. "What are you doing here?"

Especially since he'd seemed pretty

determined to avoid her earlier at the hospital. His eyes slowly rose. Still, he didn't utter a word.

"Wow. The silent treatment." She tossed up her hands. "Fine." Brushing past him, she said, "Feel free to leave at any time."

Keith grabbed her hand, the intensity of his touch stopping her instantly. She'd missed the feel of him. Missed his smell. Missed the sound of his voice. Missed his touch. Missed him period. And she hated all of it.

Tilting her head back, she blinked rapidly to rid the tears clouding her eyes. "Why are you here, Keith?" Her tone was weak, and she chastised herself for not sounding stronger.

"I need to share something with you, Sadona. Something that's hard for me to talk about."

When she glanced down at him and saw the troubled expression on her face, it clenched her heart. Whatever it was had to be serious. Inching down next to him, she waited for him to begin.

"My ex and I were only together a short time before she got pregnant. A couple of months," he said. "I never saw a future with her, but I was determined to do the right thing. Even if it were for the wrong reason."

Keith glanced at her briefly, sadness lingering in his eyes. Somehow she knew this tale wouldn't have a happy ending.

"Like any relationship, we had our ups and downs. Unfortunately, there were more downs than ups. But I wanted my son to be raised in a two-parent household."

Sadona nodded her understanding.

"We never argued in front of KJ, never gave him a reason to think mommy and daddy were unhappy. But we both were."

"Is that why you two never married?" They were together years and had a child together. Marriage seemed like a logical step. Yet, they'd never taken it. She was curious as to why.

"Marriage was never on her career path. I was okay with that, because it hadn't been on mine either."

Did that mean he wasn't keen on the idea of marriage, or simply hadn't been at the time? She wasn't sure why the idea of him rejecting marriage troubled her—especially when she, herself, had no intentions of ever marrying again—but it had.

"I'd never had any aspiration of becoming a father, but when I held KJ in my arms for the first time, I understood the concept of love at first sight. And I knew I'd move mountains for him."

The conviction on his face, in his tone, made Sadona smile.

"The day of the accident..." Keith paused a moment, looking away from her. "The day of the accident I learned the child I'd loved for seven years wasn't mine."

Stunned, Sadona gasped. "Oh my God. Keith..." She had no idea what to say.

"We'd given blood. Just in case. I'm type AB. I would have passed an A or B allele to KJ, but he was type O. There was no way I could have fathered him."

"I'm so sorry this happened to you."

"Yeah, me, too. I loved that kid like my own. I raised him like my own. To me, he was and will always be my son."

When his voice cracked, Sadona's eyes filled with tears. How could any woman do this to any man? They had to know their deception would eventually be unmasked. Keith leaned forward, rested his elbows on his thighs and pinched the bridge of his nose.

Hesitating a second, she placed her hand on his back and ironed it up and down. "Why tell me any of this, Keith?"

His head lowered. "In hopes that you will understand."

"Understand what?"

He eyed her. "Understand why I responded the way I did when I saw your ex at your place."

Sadona reclaimed her hand, a hint of anger creeping in as she recalled the way he'd treated her that day. This time she turned away and stared out into the darkness.

"Her ex was KJ's biological father. Unbeknownst to me, she'd been sleeping with us both. And when he didn't want to play daddy, she let me believe I'd fathered KJ. It's no excuse for the way I acted, but that moment took me back to when I sat in the hospital family consultation room trying the process all of the betrayal. I let my past influence me."

Keith's hands tightened into fists and he dropped his head again. They sat in silence for a long time. Rana had been right. There was heartache in Keith's past, and a lot of it. Thinking about what he'd gone through tugged at her heart.

"I'm sorry, Sadona. It shouldn't have taken so long for me to say that to you. I know I'm sorry isn't enough, and it shouldn't be. But if you don't believe anything else," he brought his gaze back to hers, "believe me when I say I love you."

The sincerity in his eyes caused her breath to hitch.

"From the moment you became mine, I've been afraid of losing you. I just never imagined I'd be the reason why. I threw us away, Sadona, and I'll regret that for the rest of my life." He stood and rushed away.

Apparently experiencing a change of heart, he stopped. A beat later, he turned and hurried back to her. She stood out of uncertainty. Keith rested his hands and either side of her neck and lowered his mouth dangerously close to hers, but he didn't kiss her. Instead, he rubbed his stubbled cheek against hers, similar to how a cat showed its human affection.

His mouth moved closer to her ear, his warm breath tingling her jaw. And when he spoke, his lips tickled her lobe.

"I am a deep feeler. Being without you is killing me. Give me another chance," he said. "I need another chance."

She closed her eyes and resisted the urge to leap into his arms. God knows she wanted to, but she couldn't forget how he'd hurt her so easily— even despite having a better understanding as to why he'd reacted the way he had.

"Please, baby," he said.

Each brush of his cheek against hers was like tiny darts laced with a potent lust elixir that intoxicated her more and more. She'd always loved the way his unshaven face felt against her. But now it was like an aphrodisiac.

His hands fell to her waist, and he pulled her closer to him. "Just one more chance."

"To do what, Keith?" she finally managed. The words came out in a near moan. She chastised herself, then sent the command to her brain to pull away from him. Of course the defiant organ ignored it.

"To love you right, Sadona. Give me another chance to love you right."

His words made her heart pitter-patter in her chest. She rested her hands against his and caressed them gently. A blink later, she pushed them away. "No."

Rearing back, Keith stared into her eyes, his expression void of any emotion. Had she stunned him as much as she'd stunned herself?

"I don't trust you, Keith," she said. "I don't trust you not to hurt me again."

Which was a lie, because foolish or not, she

did trust him and believed her heart would be safe with him. But a part of her—a petty part—needed him to feel as she'd felt for the past few weeks—abandoned by the one she loved.

With that, she climbed the stairs and escaped inside. Unfortunately, her heart wouldn't allow her to stay there—or play this childish game. Not with Keith's heart, not with their love. She wouldn't apologize for loving him the way she did, nor would she continue to deny it.

Yanking the door open, she darted out, slamming into a wall of muscle. She drew in a sharp breath, startled by Keith's presence. His strong arms wrapped around her and held her close to him.

"Keith. I assumed—"

"Do you always do that? Assume?"

Sadona thought back to when they'd first met and flashed a low-wattage smile. "I *thought* you would have been halfway to your vehicle."

"Don't think I'm going to give up that easily."

"But you did before."

"Never again." He dragged a finger down the side of her face. "Never again. I've never been more lost in my life. I don't know what to say, baby. I don't know how to go about fixing us. Help me, please. I don't want us to be a memory. I don't want to spend the rest of my life trying to forget you." He shrugged. "I'll do any and everything I have to do to make things right between us again. I don't want to lose you."

His words caressed her. "A short time ago you didn't seem overly concerned with holding on to me. *You* cut *me* loose, remember? Why the change of heart, Keith?"

"There was no change of heart, just a change in the man. I was wrong to handle things the way I did, Sadona. Finally listening to your message made me realize just how wrong I'd been. But even before that, I knew…"

"You knew what?"

"That I couldn't live without you."

Sadona swallowed hard. "I'd be lying if I said I haven't missed you like crazy. I'd also be lying if I said I wasn't still pissed at you. Running off the way you did was an asshole thing to do."

"I agree," Keith said.

"You should have given me an opportunity to explain, instead of you jumping to conclusions."

"You're right."

"Just the night before you'd told me you loved me, Keith. And I believed you. But when you treated me like I was nothing to you, I questioned whether you truly meant it or had said it because you thought it was the right thing to say." It wasn't like he hadn't done the right thing for the wrong reason before.

Keith studied her a moment. "Our eyes are the windows into our soul. That's what you told me once, right?"

Sadona nodded. "Yes."

Keith released her and took a step back. "Look

into my eyes, Sadona. Take a good, long look and tell me what you see. And if you don't see yourself there, Sadona Lassiter, you're not looking deep enough."

She stared into his intense brown eyes and a tear trickled down her cheek. Her mother's words rang in her ears. *Always choose love, especially when it's the only option*. In this case, it was. The only thing she wanted to do was love Keith and have him love her in return.

"Our hearts are aligned, Sadona Lassiter."

Sadona stood toe to toe with him. "Don't make me regret loving you, Keith Fremont. And you better get it right this time, because you won't get a third chance."

Keith rested a hand behind her neck. "I won't need one."

Somehow, she knew he was right.

Lowering his mouth to hers, they kissed foolishly. Their lips touching rejuvenated her soul. Their tongues sparred wildly, urgently, intensely. Every swipe filled her more and more until she overflowed with desire for him.

Breaking their untamed connection, Keith stared into her eyes. "I love you, sugar lips. Wherever you are, my heart will always be."

"I love you, Dr. Fremont."

And she knew she always would.

Epilogue

The one thing Keith always did without fail when he came in and found Sadona asleep on the couch was kneel beside her, lift her shirt and pepper her stomach with kisses—because it was his favorite part of her body, he'd said—then climb in behind her. Today, he'd get the surprise of his life, just as she had that morning.

Hearing his footsteps on the porch, she closed her eyes and pretended to be asleep—her usual ploy. As predicted, Keith shuffled toward her. Straying from routine, instead of lifting her shirt, he simply snuggled in behind her and kissed her exposed shoulder.

She smiled but kept her eyes shut. Keith kissed her shoulder again, then the side of her neck, then the space below her earlobe. When his warm lips brushed her ear, she shivered from the sensation.

"Marry me, Sadona Lassiter."

Sadona's lids flew open, and she whipped her head around to face Keith. "What did you just say?"

Though she'd heard him crystal clear, it was the first question to come to mind. Plus, it couldn't hurt to make sure her ears hadn't been playing tricks on her. At the magnitude of the question, her pulse kicked up a notch and her heart thumped a little harder and faster in her chest.

Keith lifted her hand and slowly kissed each finger. "I tried living without you once. It felt as if I were suffocating. I never want to feel that way again. I never want to be without you again. I want to have and to hold you for the rest of my life. I want to be your lover. I want to be your best friend. I want to be your...everything. But most importantly, I want to be your husband. I know it's only been a little over a year, but—"

"Yes," Sadona blurted. The word escaped so fast she experienced a brief ping of embarrassment. "Yes," she repeated, this time a little more controlled.

"Yes?" Keith echoed.

Sadona nodded. "Absolutely, yes."

Keith placed his hand behind her neck and kissed her senseless. When he pulled away they both fought for their next breath. Yeah, she could get used to a lifetime of these kind of kisses and definitely a lifetime with the man giving them.

"You have made me the happiest man alive. I love you, sugar lips."

"I love you, too. But..."

His brow furrowed. "But what?"

"I'm a little disappointed. You broke tradition."

Keith's expression relaxed and he laughed. "Don't worry. We'll get a ring ASAP. I wanted you to pick out exactly what you want since you'll be wearing it...forever."

His explanation warmed her soul, but that

wasn't what she had been referring to. "Yes, I will be wearing it forever, but that's not what I'm talking about. You didn't pepper my stomach with kisses." She pouted for effect. "I kinda like when you do that."

"Oh, you want belly kisses. Woman, I'll give you all the belly kisses you can handle." He lifted her shirt. "And then—" His head snapped back. "Whoa. Baby, there's something—" He stopped abruptly, fine lines etching his forehead.

"What does it say? Read it aloud."

Keith's eyes roamed over the words written on her stomach in nontoxic marker. "Dear Daddy, there wouldn't be me without you. Mommy loves you and I will, too. In a few months we will be a family. Yippee! I think that is dandy. I don't know yet if I'm a girl or a boy, but one thing for sure is I'm all yours."

Sadona sat forward and spoke gently. "Surprise, baby. You're going to be a father."

"I'm going to be—" His words hitched, making it sound as if the air had been sucked from his lungs unexpectedly.

He smiled, then donned a terrified expression. He chuckled, then sobered.

He dragged a hand over his head, then froze. His lips parted, then closed.

He scrubbed his palm back and forth over his mouth, then swallowed hard.

A blink later, he cried.

"Aww, baby," she said, her own tears flowing.

"We're having a baby?" he asked as if he just couldn't believe it.

She nodded. "Yes."

"You're having my baby?"

She nodded again. "Yes, Dr. Fremont, I'm having your baby."

Keith pulled his bottom lip between his teeth and nodded. He tried to speak, but emotions choked him. Pulling her into his arms, he held her tight, his tears wetting the crook of her neck.

"I love you. I love you. I love you. So much," he said.

"I know. And I love you, too."

They held each other for what felt like an eternity. When they finally broke apart, he rested his forehead against hers.

"I don't want to wait, Sadona. I want to marry you. Right now if I could. Promise me soon."

"Okay."

Two weekends later, they held a small ceremony by the pond in Keith's—their—backyard. There were no bridesmaids, no groomsmen, just the two of them standing before God and their closest friends and family.

She'd worn an off-the-shoulder, floor-length gentle ivory dress with a fitted bodice and plunging sweetheart neckline. Keith had worn an ivory vest, a crisp white shirt underneath and ivory pants. To say he looked handsome would have been a gross understatement.

If she hadn't been already carrying his child,

she would have come back from their honeymoon in Santorini Greece pregnant. They'd spent a ridiculous amount of time making love inside their gorgeous suite with a cliffside terrace that provided an amazing view of the Aegean Sea. When they weren't making love, they explored on scooters, toured ancient sites, hiked and shopped.

While their wedding day and honeymoon had been amazing, nothing would ever top the birth of their boys. Twins. Eric and Anthony Fremont. It had been a rough pregnancy—with her being placed on bed rest the last three months—but it had been all worth it the second she'd held their perfect little bodies for the first time. Her miracle babies.

Months after their birth, she still couldn't believe she was a mother. Dreams did come true.

"Have you ever seen anything more perfect?" she asked, eyeing their sons, guarded by their two fierce K-9 protectors.

Keith kissed the side of her head. "Yes. But these two are a close second. He directed her mouth toward his and kissed her lips gently, then cradled her face. "Thank you, my queen."

Sadona smiled at the epithet he'd used. "For what?"

"For being you. For loving me. For giving me the two most precious gifts a woman could ever give a man. For all you do for the boys and me. Woman, you are everything to us. Everything. We are damn—darn—lucky to have you. I love you beyond words, Mrs. Fremont, and I always will."

"Thank you, my king."

Keith chuckled. "For what?"

"For being the man I've always known was out there for me. For being you. A great father. A great husband. A great friend. Thank you for loving me unconditionally. For giving me two of the greatest gifts a man could ever give a woman. Thank you for all *you* do for the boys and me. Man, you are everything to me, everything to us. Everything. And we are darn lucky to have you. It's not humanly possible to show you how much you mean to me, but I promise to try every day of my life. I love you beyond words, reason and understanding, Dr. Fremont. And I always will."

THE END

ABOUT THE AUTHOR

By day, Joy Avery works as a customer service assistant. By night, the North Carolina native travels to imaginary worlds—creating characters whose romantic journeys invariably end happily ever after.

Since she was a young girl growing up in Garner, Joy knew she wanted to write. Stumbling onto romance novels, she discovered her passion for love stories. Instantly, she knew these were the type stories she wanted to pen.

Real characters. Real journeys. Real good love is what you'll find in a Joy Avery romance.

Joy is married with one child. When not writing, she enjoys reading, cake decorating, pretending to expertly play the piano, driving her husband insane, and playing with her dog.

Joy is a member of Romance Writers of America and Heart of Carolina Romance Writers.

WHERE YOU CAN FIND ME

WWW.JOYAVERY.COM
FACEBOOK.COM/AUTHORJOYAVERY
TWITTER.COM/AUTHORJOYAVERY
INSTAGRAM.COM/AUTHORJOYAVERY
PINTEREST.COM/AUTHORJOYAVERY
AUTHORJOYAVERY@GMAIL.COM

To stay in the know, visit my website to sign up for my newsletter *WINGS OF LOVE NEWSLETTER*.

Be sure to follow me on:

AMAZON
BOOKBUB

Made in the USA
Columbia, SC
27 October 2022